Sweetly Sings the Donkey

Sweetly Sings the Donkey

BY SHELAGH DELANEY

G. P. Putnam's Sons

New York

Sweetly sings the donkey
As he goes to grass
He who sings so sweetly
Is sure to be an ass.

Contents

Sweetly Sings the Donkey

Sweetly Sings the Donkey

I am here and I am safe and I am sick of it. How long have I been here? How much longer must I stay? This Convalescent Home is overrun by nuns. Hundreds of nuns. They are supposed to be taking care of the thirty girls convalescing here. The eldest girl is fourteen. The youngest six. Some of them have been here for years and they don't look any healthier than I do now so if this convalescent place does me as much good as it seems to have done them it's hopeless and I've had it. Most of the girls sleep in dormitories with twelve beds in each but a few of us are privileged and have private rooms. My private room is very small at the top of this big house. For furniture I have one bed, one cupboard so big that all my belongings don't fill one of its drawers, and a lame chair. The room is on the sea-facing side of the house so I have a good view of the ocean. The windows are iron-barred like in loony bins. Although the place is so religious, its owners have taken no notice of Jesus Christ's warnings about putting up houses on sand, for this building has been put up on the beach and the downstairs rooms get flooded out every high tide and all surrounding the house, and we inside it are shifting sandhills that cause the creeps—

—I can't find out where the nuns sleep. This might seem a stupid thing to bother about like imagining the King and Queen having a bath or going to the lav but I'm not the only person here who thinks stupid things because all the new girls are wondering the same. We have searched the Home for nun cells but no go. Out on the cold beach this morning getting our fresh air we discussed it and somebody suggested that the reason why we can't find any nun cells is because there aren't any on account of the nuns having taken a vow to stay awake all the time. This was ridiculed but when you come to think it's not so daft really—not when you consider some of the other vows nuns make. Late on last night I investigated the cellars—not mainly to discover the nuns' hiding places but just for the sake of investigation. The cellars I found out are filled with food supplies. Sacks of spuds turnips carrots and onions. Flourbins and

●

breadbins. Giant-size tins of National Dried Milk and powdered egg. Salt and sugar and jars of malt and bottles of orange juice and cod-liver oil and green pills for constipation. But no nuns. It's a mystery. I think they sleep hanging upside down from the roof rafters. They all look ghostly pale and faded. Everybody here looks pale and faded, for that matter—all the children are sickly—some are recovering and some will never recover and we are all either too thin or too fat, too tall or too short. Every morning we are weighed and carefully measured. I am the tallest thinnest girl in the place and they are trying to build me up by stuffing me with iron pills brown malt cod-liver oil, and bottles of Scott's Emulsion, with so many vitamins piling up inside me I'm bound to explode sooner or later into a mushroom cloud—

—very young nun who is new here. She is not pale and faded. She comes out with us when we go to the beach and if the weather is windy and cold she gets very rosy cheeks which makes a nice change after seeing so many white faces. When we were throwing a ball about this morning she joined in the game. She can run fast but I don't know how with all the long robes she has to wear. They flap around her ankles and get under her feet. The wind blew so hard once while she chased the ball that I hoped it would blow her hood off but it didn't. I was sorry. It would have been interesting to see what a bald-

•

headed woman looks like. The more she ran the redder
her cheeks got and a man watching us couldn't take his
eyes off her. I can't make out why she wants to be a nun.
She could get hundreds of lads if she wanted. Still—
maybe she doesn't want—

—has stopped coming out with us now and seems to
have disappeared. This is just the place for people to
disappear from. So the young nun has gone and the old
nuns take us to the beach now. They don't do any harm.
They just sit and watch to make sure we don't do anything they won't like. One of them's got a face that looks
like it doesn't like anything. She wears glasses and walks
as if she's wearing iron pants. I think she is one of the
bosses. When we first arrived here she told us the rules.
She thinks we are frightened of her and has the habit of
staring at you as if trying to fix you with the evil eye.
She stared at me once for so long that when she finally
turned her eyes away I asked her if she was sure she had
seen enough. Every night before going to bed we are
given one hour to write letters and to read books from
the library. Next door to our reading room is a big
library full of books that look interesting but we are
not allowed to read them and must make do with the
children's books from the glass-fronted cupboard but
they are all children's adventure books which I read
years ago and didn't like even then. The Chief Nun who
has an office all to herself has given me a Bible to read

instead. I told her I had read it but she said: "It will do you no harm to read it again and in all probability will do you some good."

So I'm going through it chapter by chapter. It seems a waste to read it when there is a room full of books I haven't read next door but there's nothing I can do about it. They don't get newspapers here. No wireless. IT IS FORBIDDEN to buy comics. IT IS FORBIDDEN to run. IT IS FORBIDDEN to sing loudly. IT IS FORBIDDEN to read and IT IS FORBIDDEN to write outside the lawful times. My fountain pen has been taken from me and put into the Chief Nun's secret drawer for safekeeping. I am only allowed to have it once a day and the way it is treated you'd think it was a valuable relic. To keep us occupied on bad-weather days when we can't go outside we are allowed to sew. I can sew and if we were set to make something useful then I wouldn't mind doing it but instead of sewing skirts shirts frocks or blouses we are set to make nightdress cases. When I think of what I could be doing instead, I get upset. There we all sit in one big room threading our needles and licking our cotton while a hawk-eyed nun keeps us under observation, every now and again offering a bit of advice in connection with the hemming of hems and the stitching of seams. Conversation is permitted but most of the girls watch their tongues in case they say something the Nun-in-Charge won't like so we sit hushed up sometimes whispering:

"Can I lend your scissors?"

"May I borrow your black cotton?"

This afternoon I leaned across the table to the girl sitting opposite and whispered:

"There's a black beetle crawling in your hair."

She screamed.

I asked once if instead of sewing I could write or read but the answer was NO. I decided to go on strike and put my tools down.

"What are you doing?" the nun inquired.

"Thinking."

"What about?"

"The Sufferings of St. John of the Cross."

They clicked their tongues inside their heads and said: "The Devil finds work for idle hands." And forced me to pick my sewing up again. It's true I suppose that the Devil does find work for idle hands but he finds work for idle thoughts too and idle thoughts can be just as dangerous, if they are left lying about. My head is crammed with idle thoughts I've had and there seems no way of letting them out. The contents of my head will soon be like a rubbish tip and some rubbish tips I've known have festered first then burst out into flames. I am getting bored with having to read the Bible while there is a room full of books next door I've never read.

•

But that's the way it is. The books are in prison just like me—

—girl got a food parcel from home this morning. It was full of biscuits and chocolate and toffees. A month's toffee coupons at least. And the nuns made the poor girl share the contents out with all the girls who share her dormitory. It was tragic. The girl looked as if she'd have a heart attack as she doled out all her treasures. I don't think it's good to force us to be unselfish. It only makes you selfish when you get older and can please yourself. The girl hated being forced to give her sweets away and all the girls she had to give them to didn't really enjoy eating what they were given. If she'd been left alone she'd probably have handed some of the stuff round of her own free will and that way she'd have enjoyed it and so would the others. We are wondering whether the nuns read our letters before they post them. Some old-timers say they do and some say they don't. The best thing's to find out for ourselves—

—morning we went for a walk on the beach. The ocean was a long way away. We could hardly see it. The sun was shining but the sand was frozen solid. I've never been to the seaside in winter. It is lonely and quiet in a way I have never come across before. While we were walking we saw a man on a horse. They came over the sandhills and galloped fast along the beach. The man wore brown leather boots right up to his knees. He

●

19

looked very handsome. I hope I see him again before I
leave this place. It must be nice to ride a horse. Better
than donkeys. One of the girls staying here says she has
a pony and rides it every day when she is at home. I
think she tells lies though. Yesterday she told me her
father was tortured to death in a Japanese Prisoner of
War Camp but this morning after we'd been given our
letters she was telling everybody she had got a letter
from him and when I asked her how she managed to
get letters from ghosts she said it's her mother who's
dead. Tomorrow she'll be bereft of both parents. If she
was a real orphan she wouldn't like it because she's the
most spoilt girl I've ever known. She has dozens of frocks
and hundreds of pairs of shoes and necklaces and bangles
and brooches. She moans about the food we get here and
it's not all that bad really. It's a lot better than she gets
at home I'll bet. She is very pleased at being ill and does
all sorts of things to make herself iller and gain as much
sympathy as she can from the nuns, who put her to bed
whenever she complains about a pain or a sickly feeling.
I never knew anyone who enjoys lying in bed so much
as she does. If you let her she will tell you all the diseases
she's had—whooping cough chicken pox measles scarlet
fever diphtheria croup bronchitis pneumonia. And she's
always showing off her appendicitis scar which isn't
worth showing off anyway. I've had worse scars left over
from cat scratches. She's dead marred and cries if you

●

look at her sometimes. I told her that the garden at the
back of the house is haunted by the restless spirit of a
man who used to work in it and who cut off his own
head with a pair of gardening shears. I told her how he
roams at night making terrible moans which come out of
his severed head which he carries before him in his up-
turned cap. She was scared stiff, and cried all night. She
didn't tell the nuns why she was frightened which is a
pity because if they found out they might have me sent
home. I wish they would.

For tea today we had bread and black-currant jam
washed down with a cup of cocoa. It was very good but
at home it would only be considered a fill-in for between
proper meals. I would sooner have the sort of teas we
have at home and could just eat a plate of potato pie
gravy red cabbage and apple crumble and custard. It is
terrible to feel hungry all the time and if I stay here
much longer I'll look like a skeleton—

—life gets no better and no worse. If it did one or the
other, things would be livened up a bit. The Horseman
rides every day on the beach now. All the girls here are
going around saying they love him but if he loves anyone it is either a nun called Sister Veronica or me. When
we are out walking I walk beside her at the end of the
line. The Horseman always smiles at us two but I don't
think it's me he's after. Sister Veronica is not like the
other nuns. She doesn't wear glasses and although she's

pale she looks as if she's got some life in her. She's not old or young but somewhere in between. I have made friends with a girl called Nina Tarragon who is staying here convalescing after rheumatic fever. The name Tarragon is a new one on me and is the name of an herb she says. I like her and we get on well together which is a good job because neither of us gets on very well with anyone else. Most of the other girls are childish, even the girls who are older than we are. They make me laugh sometimes the way they carry on, and some of the things they say are very strange. One of them was telling us yesterday that Negro men can only have sexual intercourse six times in their lives and that if they have it seven times they die. She also tells a lot of jokes which I mainly fell out of my cradle laughing at—

—church services every morning after breakfast. Every morning. Once a week is enough for me and sometimes that can be once too often. I have been trying to think of ways I can get out of going but can't come up with anything that the Chief Nun will accept. Two girls are allowed to stay away because they are Spiritualists—or at any rate their parents are—

—this morning during the service while the incense was being swung in its burner I collapsed in a dead faint. Sister Veronica carried me from the church and laid me out on my bed. She stood over me until I came to consciousness and we looked at each other. I moaned.

●

"What's the matter with you?" Sister Veronica inquired.

"I don't know," I said—

—same thing happened again and again Sister Veronica carried me away.

"What's the matter this time?" she inquired.

"I don't know," I said.

"The doctor will soon find out," she announced and smiled.

So they sent for the doctor and while he was coming I imagined myself paler and weaker on the bed. The doctor finished examining me and rocked about on the lame chair by my bed. He tapped his fountain pen against his buck teeth and then got up.

"Anything serious?" Sister Veronica asked.

He moved away from the bed and spoke to her in a low voice by the window:

"An overactive imagination. She's very highly strung and finds it hard to relax physically and mentally. You know how it is with some children—especially children who've been very ill—they dwell on certain things and create images they can't control. I'd keep her in bed for a day or two and let her rest completely and keep her away from the church until she's a bit stronger. A lot of children—especially young girls who are developing—get obsessions. Sometimes with sex, sometimes it's religion—

●

it's an outlet for their energy and it can become quite a problem if it isn't handled carefully from the outset."

He picked up his bag and said good-bye. So there it is. I don't have to go to the church until I'm stronger in mind and body—

—if I have to stay in bed much longer I really will go daft. I haven't seen anybody for days. The only visitor I have is Sister Veronica who brings me food and drink and although she doesn't ever say it I know she thinks I'm a big fraud.

"Could I have something to read?" I asked her once.

"You have the Bible," she said. "That should satisfy you."

And it does but only so far—

"Can't I have any visitors? I've not got anything that's catching."

"I'm not so sure about that," she replied and took my empty plates away—

—allowed a visitor. Tarragon came and we were allowed to eat together.

"Anything interesting happened?" I asked her.

"No. Nothing. What's wrong with you?"

"It's a mystery."

"Rumors're going round."

"What are they?"

"Somebody told me you have epileptic fits."

"And what did you say?"

●

24

"I told them you'd been having visions in the church."

She hardly ever smiles this girl and I often wonder whether she always feels as mournful and serious as she looks. We ate our boiled beef and carrots—

"My room isn't like this one. Why have you got iron bars up at the windows?"

"It's to stop me from flinging myself through the glass down onto the rocks—"

—walking all day long and for once I feel tired enough to sleep well. Instead of walking on the beach we went along the main road and nearly reached the city. I didn't realize how many other convalescent homes there are around here. On top of the highest hill is a sanatorium for T.B. patients. One of the places is for old men and we saw some of the old men strolling along two by two just like we do when we're out. I feel bad enough walking along the streets in a procession, so what they felt like being so ancient I don't know and to make matters worse they all had labels looped through their buttonholes with their names and addresses written on them. This is something even we don't have to put up with and it is rotten to see old men going about like that. It's humiliating if you ask me. I could understand it if they were all soft in the head but they seemed sane enough to me—one of them whose hair must have been ginger when he was younger kept stepping out of line and once he nearly got run over by a double-decker bus. He'd been collecting bits of evergreens and had a bunch of them in his hand including a small pine branch which was thick with cones. The man in charge of the old men was full of his own importance and kept giving orders in a loud voice so that passersby would know he was the Boss. I've seen the same thing happen at school when a girl is made a prefect or a games captain. They change in front of your eyes and start to strut. —Strutting is all very well but if you need a special badge to flash around before you can strut you're not a natural strutter and everyone knows it. Trouble is not everyone lets on they know it and they're just as bad in their way as the artificial strutters. The Young Man in charge of Old Men kept ordering the gingery one to get in line and behave but he took no notice. He played hopscotch on the flagstones and had a few words with a tree he met on the way. And then he did the thing that nearly had me dead with laughing. He unfastened his flybuttons and peed up against the wall like lads do. We were rushed away and one girl said it was disgusting and he ought to be locked up and only dogs do things like that and so I suppose she's right and he was an old dog—

—at long last I've been given a book to read. Sister Veronica brought it to me and she looked ashamed when she handed it over. It is called *Dot and Go One* or *The Good Shepherd's Care* and is written by someone called

M. Blanche Hayward. It is published by the Religious
Tract Society—

—storm blew last night. This house is too close to the
sea for comfort. I watched the lightning from my bedroom window. The sea chopped against the bottom end
of the house and if it had chopped a bit harder we'd have
all fell down. Early this morning was chaos. The cellar
and all the rooms on the ground floor were smothered in
water and the nuns with their skirts tucked up and their
sleeves rolled high baled out and mopped up for all they
were worth. This afternoon a few of us—the tough ones
able to stand up to the hard weather—went to the beach
with Sister Veronica. We found all sorts of stuff washed
up on the sand and the man who does professional
beachcombing was already at business and from the
sound of it seemed to be finding all kinds of treasures
and bargains. He chuckled and laughed and rubbed his
hands together and his sack was packed out tight so that
his back bent double under the weight of it. We found
a shipwrecked armchair standing up on its legs and facing the sea like a throne. We found old bombshells and
bits of shrapnel and big pieces of metal that might have
come off a sunken ship or gunned-down plane and tin
cans, rusty oildrums and stacks of wood, wellybobs and
dead birds and a lot of other dead things we couldn't
identify. It was very interesting. The beachcomber was
nearly off his head with happiness by the time every-

●

thing had been inspected. Another man came walking along the shore. He smiled at us and at Sister Veronica.

"Good morning, Sister," he said and raised his cap.

I didn't recognize him at first then all of a sudden the penny dropped. The man who usually rides the brown horse. He ought never to get off his horse because without it he isn't much to go mad about. It is a pity that he isn't as beautiful as I had thought from a distance. I always hoped that one day he would gallop along the beach straight through the front door of the Convalescent Home up the stairs and into the church where he would see Sister Veronica and snatch her up and carry her off under his arm to a more interesting life; but now I've had a closer look at him I don't think he'll ever do anything like that and Sister Veronica will do better to stay a Bride of Christ after all. I asked Nina if she thought the horseman was a disappointment. She said that she had never thought much about him to tell the truth as she isn't man-mad. She was sitting on the old armchair staring at the sea and fancying herself as Neptune's Daughter but she didn't get a chance to fancy herself for long because the chair was soaked and crusted with sea things and Sister Veronica, who'd been busy talking to the man and forgetful of her duties, suddenly noticed and shifted her off it quick. As we all walked along the shore the beachcomber following behind sang a song to himself:

●

Sweetly Sings the Donkey

"o crabs and crayfish prawns and shrimps
sandhoppers woodlice and lobsters beware
we'll boil you alive till you're juicy and pink
and impale all you winkles on chrome-plated pins
we'll masticate masticate thirty-two times
smacking our lips with glee
then we'll greedily gobble you up in a tick
and you'll wish you'd stayed in the depths of the sea
o you crabs and crayfish prawns and shrimps
sandhoppers woodlice and lobsters beware—

And so on and so forth. At the first pier we stopped.
Everybody else did anyway. I was so occupied listening
to what the comber was singing that I went waltzing on
straight ahead till I sank down to my knees in black mud
swamp. To wash the stuff off my legs I had to stand in a
rock pool which was high enough for me to look over the
seawall at the seaside city shut up for winter. When we
came here last summer for a day's outing the city was
open and swarmed with people. Wherever you looked
you'd be sure to see somebody having a good time and
the courting couples who lay on the beach were so engrossed in each other that they didn't notice when playing children kicked up sand all over them. But not now.

"Back home now," Sister Veronica called and we all
turned to go. The horseless sat on a rock smoking a cigarette and watched while we filed past him.

●

29

"Don't stare at him," Sister Veronica said.

"He's staring at me," I told her.

"Don't flatter yourself."

"He must be staring at you then.

> *"If you become a Nun, dear*
> *A Friar I will be*
> *In any cell you run dear*
> *Pray look behind for me,"*

I recited.

"Do you know your prayers as well as you know your jingles?" she inquired.

"Pierce O most sweet Lord Jesus Christ my inmost soul with the most joyous and healthful wound of thy love, with true serene and most apostolic charity that my soul may ever languish and melt with love and longing for thee, that it may yearn for thee and faint for thy courts and long to be dissolved and to be with thee. Grant that my soul may hunger after thee, the bread of angels, the refreshment of holy souls—"

"Are you a Catholic?"

"No."

"How do you come to know that then?"

"My father's a Catholic. I often read his Missal."

"What religion is your mother?"

"Church of England."

"Which faith were you baptized in?"

"I haven't been baptized."

"Do you ever go to church?"

"Every week."

"A Catholic or Protestant church?"

"Some weeks I feel Catholic and some weeks I feel Protestant."

"So you go to either church?"

"Yes."

"Do the priests of these churches know?"

"I don't think the priests ever see me. And if they did they wouldn't see me again because there's so many churches where I live I can go to a different one every day. No one gets a chance to know my face."

"And do you faint in these churches?"

"No."

"Then why do you faint in our church?"

"I don't know."

"Do your parents go to church regularly?"

"No. Do yours?"

"No."

"So you don't get it from them?"

"Get what?"

"Being a nun."

"No."

"Do you ever see your parents? Is it allowed?"

"Sometimes. The order I belong to isn't the strictest order."

"Do they like you being a nun?"

"No."

"How long have you been one?"

"Six years."

"I've never talked to a nun before."

"Is it strange to do so now?"

"Do you know what people are supposed to do when they see a nun coming towards them?"

"No."

"They're supposed to unfasten their coats and to keep them unfastened till they see a four-footed animal. Then it's safe to fasten your coat up again."

"And what's that ritual in aid of?"

"It's got something to do with letting the Holy Ghost in. I don't know how much truth there is in it but it's the custom."

"It must be a difficult custom to keep here. You're surrounded with nuns."

"I know. It's very bad luck not to keep the custom, but we can't keep it here."

"So what do you think will happen?"

"Something terrible probably."

"Haven't you got another custom that will cancel out the evil effects of this one?"

"I'll have to invent one."

●

"I'm sure you will."

"Is that your wedding ring?"

"Yes."

"My grandmother had a beautiful wedding ring but it had to be buried with her. It was very valuable and she'd pawned it many a time herself and wanted somebody else to have the same benefits but her fingers swelled and they would have had to chop her hand off to get it so they didn't bother. Did you have a vision?"

"What sort of a vision?"

"Joan of Arc heard voices."

"I'm not Joan of Arc."

"It's the same sort of thing, though. A man who works with my dad had three wives and ten children and last year he went to the police and confessed he was a bigamist because he said he'd heard voices telling him to repent. But no one believed him and he was sent to prison. Most people said he'd given himself up because he was sick of having three wives but I think it was just bad luck. Three wives and ten children add up to thirteen and thirteen's an unlucky number."

"If he'd taken another wife he'd have been all right you think?"

"He might."

"Are all children as superstitious as you?"

"Don't you believe in it?"

"No."

"A lot of people do. One of my aunties bought a piece of iron when she was in Lourdes last year that's supposed to come from one of the nails they nailed Jesus Christ to his cross with."

"If all the bits of iron said to have come from the nails they nailed Christ to the Cross with were collected together on this island the whole of England, Scotland and Wales would disappear beneath the ocean."

"A girl near us at home had whooping cough at Christmas and her mother cured her by making her eat a fried mouse."

"A mouse?"

"Yes."

"Cured her?"

"A mouse fried in butter."

"Fried in faith too."

"The mother said it was the mouse. What are nuns for, Sister Veronica?"

"Do we seem completely useless?"

"You do useful things I know like looking after the sick and things but you don't need to be a nun to do that so I think you must get up to something else."

"We pray."

"All the time?"

"All the time. Somewhere in the world at all hours of the day and night a nun or a monk is praying for the

souls of men. Why are you looking at me so suspi-
ciously?"

"I didn't know I was."

"You always have a funny look in your eyes."

"I must have been born with it."

"You must," she said and tripped up over the hem of
her long black robe— "O it's a long road leading them
Home," she muttered.

"Yes it is but if it was any shorter it wouldn't reach
the front door—"

I deserved the sad look she gave me. It wasn't very
funny—

—to the city this morning with Nina. We went to have
our aching teeth pulled. Sister Veronica took us. We
traveled there on a bus and it was like going through a
place where the plague has been as the inhabitants all
seem to be hiding themselves. Every shop is shuttered.
All along the promenade deck chairs are piled up and
covered with tarpaulins. It was a relief though to get off
the bus because an old man sitting behind us was cough-
ing his heart up. When we left the bus Sister Veronica
took hold of our hands and flew, dragging us off our feet
almost. We fluttered behind caught in her slip stream
and couldn't see a thing hardly because her robes bil-
lowed round our heads like giant bat-wings. One amuse-
ment arcade was open and I noticed one boy banging a
punchball against a clock, testing his strength. We nearly

trampled a shawled old man in a bathchair to death and once, just once, we stopped. But not for breath. A dignified procession of funeral cars passed by and Sister Veronica stood still on the curbstone muttering to herself until it was out of sight. Then we were off again. I glanced behind once and was sure I saw the Devil himself chasing us on a motor bike. And then we arrived at the dentist's shop.

"Come in. Come in. I've been waiting for you," the dentist said and rubbed his hands together. "Who's first?"

"Not me," said Nina.

"Not me," said I.

So we tossed a coin for it and she went in before me. There's nothing worse than waiting sometimes—it wasn't like waiting for Christmas or birthdays to come. When Nina came out of the surgery I looked at her face and went pale.

"Next customer, please."

Sister Veronica pushed me through the door and before I had time to think I was in the chair with the dentist poking instruments into my mouth.

"Now I'm going to tap each tooth individually with this small hammer and when I tap the tooth that's hurting, you tell me."

A scream's as good as any word I suppose and the dentist set to work. He pulled and pushed and twisted.

●

"Dear me, dear me, dear me," he said and his nurse wiped sweat out of his eyes. "I've pulled teeth out of the heads of buck niggers with half this trouble."

When the tooth did come out it tore my gums open and blood poured from the wound everywhere.

"Never mind now, my dear. A stitch in time will soon put that right."

The gap in my gum must have been giant-size because it took him hours to darn the hole over and even then the blood got through so that I had to keep emptying my mouth of it. The dentist examined the pulled tooth and declared it a rare specimen. To me it looked like something that had dropped out of the mouth of the prehistoric monster's skeleton in Hope Hall Museum at home.

"Would you like to keep it, my dear, as a souvenir?"

"No, thank you."

Not likely. Just the look of it gave me a pain. As I was leaving the dentist's room the nurse told me to hold out my hand and into it she dropped a bag of humbugs.

"That's for being so brave."

Sister Veronica was not impressed by my braveness though, and as soon as we were out on the street she took the toffees away from me and dropped them all into a litter bin.

"A stupid thing for a dentist to give to anybody. I look forward to the day when all children go into shops and instead of asking for bars of chocolate and sticks of toffee ask for a carrot or an apple," she said. "Your teeth must already be in the last stages of total decay."

We had to wait fifteen minutes at the bus station for our bus back to the Home and the three of us sat on a wooden bench in the waiting room. We didn't speak. My mouth was filling up with blood and I could tell from the expression on Nina's face that hers was too. A woman with a fat Pekingese dog on her knee stared at us rudely until we both spat our blood out into our handkerchiefs. After that she moved away to sit beside an open window. An old lady came into the room with a little boy. The pair of them were loaded down with bags and the lady looked exhausted. We sat behind them on the bus and both of us and the rest of the travelers admired the old lady's beautiful hair which was piled up on top of her head in waves and plaits and thick curls.

"I hope I have hair like that when I'm as old as she is," Nina said.

The rocking of the bus gradually rocked the lady to sleep and soon her head drooped to one side. The little boy fidgeted and looked around for something to do. He reached toward the woman's head and lifted her beautiful hair up so that we all could see the pink bald scalp beneath it. When he thought we'd seen enough he put the wig back and woke her.

"We get off here, Gran."

•

"Aren't you getting a clever boy," she said serenely and led him gently away.

Back at the Convalescent Home we were treated like real invalids and made to lie down for the afternoon in the sickroom which is made of glass and nothing else.

"Now you two rest here. No talking, either," Sister Veronica ordered and left us alone.

I looked across at Nina stretched out on her bed. She was wearing her sunglasses as usual.

"Would you like me to make certain that when you die you are buried wearing your sun-specs?" I asked.

"You might be the one who's buried first," she said and looked gloomier than ever.

I say she looked gloomy but that's wrong really. It isn't so much that you can see her gloominess as feel it. I tried to sleep but the sound of her breathing kept me awake, so I asked her to breathe more quietly.

"I'll stop breathing altogether if you like so's not to disturb your afternoon rest," she offered.

"What you so nowty for?"

"I'm not nowty," she snarled and sat up straight and took her sunglasses off and glared.

"O no. You don't look it," I told her and yawned against the wall.

"I don't like being disturbed," she growled.

"I don't like being disturbed either and your heavy breathing was disturbing me."

"It's a pity for you."

"Yes, it is."

"That's the trouble with you. You're too selfish."

"Go back to your heavy breathing."

"Have you ever seen anybody dead?"

"No. Have you?"

"No. I thought you might have done."

"Why?"

"I don't know."

"There's no need to bite my head off."

"I'd need a big mouth to do that."

"You're morbid, aren't you?"

"Yes."

"My grandmother died."

"But you didn't see her?"

"Wouldn't let me. They let all her relations who hadn't seen her for years while she was living have a look but not me. I used to share a bedroom with her as well. I didn't like doing that, though. I'd sooner have been on my own."

"Did she breathe heavy?"

"Heavier than you."

"I bet you were glad then when she died."

"O I danced a jig in celebration."

"I wonder what they do to people when they die?"

"Have a special man to do it anyway."

"The undertaker's man."

●

"The Egyptians make dead people into mummies."

"I've seen one of them in a museum."

"So have I. Not much really, are they?"

"They'd be interesting with their bandages off."

"I heard that the undertaker's man takes all the insides of dead people away."

"You mean all their livers and kidneys and lungs?"

"And their blood and bones too."

"What happens to all the stuff they take out then?"

"What happens to animals' insides? Have you never had stuffed sheep's heart or blood sausage?"

"No. I don't eat things like that. I once tried to eat a lamp chop but I couldn't bear cutting the meat off the bone. Then chewing it. It's bestial."

"The man next door to us died a year ago last Pancake Tuesday and me and this lad wanted to see him but they'd nailed the coffin lid down."

"Perhaps he wasn't fit to be seen."

"He was very ugly but people can't help the faces they're born with.

"The nearest thing I ever saw to dead people was in a film about concentration camps. Kids weren't meant to see this film but we got in the picture house. But when we saw it we were sorry we had because it gave us nightmares for weeks. It was about the Jews in Belsen and I've never seen anything so rotten. It showed you the gas ovens the Germans burnt the Jews in but the Jews who hadn't got burnt were all standing about. They were thin like matchstick men—you could see their bones through their flesh as well as if the flesh wasn't there. It was horrible. I don't think proper dead ones could look worse than them. And once when I was young my mother took me to see my dad who'd been sent home from abroad to a hospital near Bristol. He'd been wounded. The hospital was full of Yank soldiers who'd been wounded as well and they made a fuss over me, giving me things I'd never seen before."

"What?"

"O you know—big bars of chocolate and tins of peanuts and piles of Yankee chewing gum. They loaded me down with presents. I'd never had so much before and I bet I never have as much again. But they were all wounded and some of them had no legs and some of them had no arms and one man only had his head left attached to his body. I was scared of seeing my dad in case he was like that. But d'you know, I didn't recognize him when we reached his bed. I'd only ever seen photos of him before and on them he was big and tough and his hair was thick black."

"Why didn't you recognize him?"

"Because he was thin and white. His hair was gray and long like a girl's. All my insides heaved when I saw him. I was scared of touching him, he looked so frail."

"But he didn't die?"

•

"No. What you so interested for anyway?"

"Don't know. I just am. Do you believe in ghosts?"

"I know a lot of ghost stories."

"Not true ones."

"True ones."

"I've heard some of your true stories. You make them all up."

"They're all based on the truth. Have you noticed that big house over the road from this one?"

"I'd have to be blind not to."

"There's a woman lives there who's a witch. I've watched her at nighttimes. She sometimes changes her appearance—"

"Pull the other leg. It's got bells on it."

"But her favorite disguise is a black toad. So be careful when you go to bed tonight and watch out for a black toad to come hopping over the fence and up the stairs to get you. She's very fond of young girls with golden hair."

"What will she do if she gets me?"

"I'm not sure but she's very partial to a feast of roasted babies every now and again. I've seen her chief imp cooking them up for her supper."

"Do you have dreams?"

"Yes."

"Scaring ones?"

"Sometimes. Usually I dream I'm flying or floating through the air somehow or other."

"I have dreams but they're always frightening. One dream I have every night. It's not scaring because of murderers or robbers or things like that. It's always that I get off a train and walk along a path—it's always in the country, too—"

"Have you ever lived in the country?"

"In the war I did. My mother and father were in London and I was sent to a big old house miles away from anywhere."

"Do you know all about country things?"

"What do you mean?"

"Names of trees and birds and things like that."

"Yes."

"I'd like to know things like that. I know a bit from books but it's not the same as living it, is it?"

"I used to ride ponies bareback when I was little."

"And when you have your dream do you dream about that?"

"No. It's funny. I walk along this lane and then I find a bike and I ride it up to a house and then I get off the bike and walk into this house. It's very big and nice but there's only me in it and all of a sudden I reach the end of the house and there's no windows. Just a brick wall. It doesn't sound frightening but it is. There's nothing you can do about dreaming, is there?"

●

"Except to stay awake all night and day."

"I've tried that but it's no good."

"Are you hungry?"

"It's no use you asking for food. They'll only give you bread in hot milk because of your sore mouth."

"I want something I can bite."

"Well, don't look at me," she said and started to polish her sun-specs carefully on the bedsheet.

I have now finished reading *Dot and Go One* or *The Good Shepherd's Care*. Everything in the story turned out for the best—

—fat nun here who is asking for trouble the way she carries on. They say fat people are jolly and happy but in her case I think it's more happy-daft than anything else. Her face haunts me. She laughs at everything— even things that aren't the least bit funny and her face is fixed in a horrible grin. The sound of her being cheerful can be heard miles away and I'm sure ships at sea often mistake it for a foghorn. She is determined to be cheerful at all costs but she spreads misery and gloom and causes more hatred than Hitler. We went for a walk this morning and for once the sun was shining and I was feeling fine and enjoying myself in my own way but—

"What's that gloomy face for?" the fat nun asked.

"What gloomy face?"

"This one," she said and pinched my cheek between her finger and thumb.

●

45

I looked at her.

"Come on, child. Give us a smile. You've got a lovely smile. Don't be niggardly with it. Put a twinkle in your dark eyes."

All the happiness I had been feeling started to run away from me and I didn't blame it. If I'd been able to I'd have run away myself.

"What have you got to be gloomy about a fine day like this?"

She only asks questions so she can answer them herself so I walked along like someone struck dumb.

"The rain has stopped. The sun is up. Let the sunshine into your soul, child."

I nearly asked her to play another gramophone record. The more she said the more miserable I began to feel and all the sad things that have happened to me, that I have heard of or imagined, came into my mind and a song I once heard Billie Holiday sing started to sing itself in my head—

Sunday is gloomy my hours are slumberless
Dearest the shadows I live with are numberless
Little white flowers will never awaken you
Not where the black coach of sorrow has taken you

O I wished then that the black coach of sorrow would take the fat nun away—

•

—while the others were in church I went to the kitchen to see the woman who does the cooking here. She was peeling onions and the fumes had the pair of us in tears. It is a good idea to get friendly with people who have food under their control. This woman has taken a fancy to me and gives me things. I collected today six arrow-root biscuits, cocoa and sugar in a twist of paper and a chunk of slab cake. She has warned me to keep quiet about it though, because the nuns disapprove of favoritism. We had an interesting talk mainly about my fainting attack in the church. According to the cook this is a sure sign that my soul is rebelling against the false chains of religion that society wants to bind it with. She comes from a Roman Catholic family but has renounced the faith as in her opinion after giving the matter thought and consideration religion as a whole is an evil influence that the upper classes encourage among the working classes to keep them from rising. In her opinion the nearest thing to God is Vladymir Ilyitch Lenin of Russia and Josef Stalin. She says too that though the nuns are good decent women in some ways they are no better than the ancient druids who worshiped pagan gods at Stonehenge. When I asked her how feeling the way she does about religion she can bring herself to work in a place as religious as this she answered:

"Needs must when the Devil drives."

While she was talking I saw propped up on the shelf

above her kitchen sink a book called *The Manifesto of the Communist Party*. Noticing that I had seen it she said that I would do well to read it soon before they get at me because they are only out to oppress and exploit the class I come from for their own ends. According to her, only a revolution will ever bring true democracy to this country and the sooner revolution comes (she said) the better, and even though hundreds of innocents will be slaughtered they will die in a good cause and men must be willing to sacrifice themselves. But that depends I suppose on which men you're thinking of—

—house is very quiet at night or so it might seem to some people but every noise sounds ten times louder than it is and near noises seem far away and far noises seem near. But all the sounds of here are strange to me. How in a city do you get to know the noise of the sea and hooting owls at the same time or any time? How in a city do you get used to tree branches tapping at your bedroom windows and creaking horribly in the night? Once I got to know what these and all the other strange sounds are they didn't worry me but all the same it would be nice to hear something familiar. Many a time I imagine some of the noises I know and see things and remember things of sirens and searchlights, gas mask and shelter, ours and theirs going over, all-clear. Back to bed again. Street parties and flags out flying for victory. All smiles. School. 1 2 3 pussy went to pee. Norman

●

Conquest 1066. Henry the Eighth had six wives. I wandered lonely as a cloud that floats on high.

"Geography is that field of learning in which the characteristics of particular places on the earth's surface are examined. The face of the earth is made up of many different kinds of features each one the momentary result of an ongoing process. Your attention please, young woman!" the teacher said.

"I believe in God the Father Almighty Maker of Heaven and Earth and in Jesus Christ his only Son our Lord who was born of the Virgin Mary suffered under Pontius Pilate was crucified dead and buried the third day he rose again from the dead."

"Now altogether, girls—Books of the Bible," the same teacher said.

"Genesis Exodus Leviticus NUMBERS!

Deuteronomy Joshua Judges Ruth!"

Has worked hard this term. Does not exert herself sufficiently. Unwilling to accept discipline. Has some originality of thought. A likable girl. Inclined to sullenness. Uncommunicative. Overimaginative. Has difficulty distinguishing fact from fiction. This girl is a liar. Expect improvement next term. Position in class examinations ninth. Number of children in class, 52. Times absent—ten. Times late—forty-three. This will not do. O beware the moonlight shining upon your sleeping face. It causes madness. O beware the black beetle crawling

●

across the toe of your boot. He warns a death. O beware the stare of a cross-eyed woman. Spit three times on the ground to break the bad luck she brings. O beware you who have stolen graystone chippings off a tomb. You bring a curse down on yourself forever. May Day Molly Dancers beg a penny for a song. . . .

Bus-ticket numbers reckon up fortunes—1 for sorrow 2 for joy 3 for a letter 4 for a boy 5 for silver 6 for gold 7 for a secret that's never been told. The nice girl says I LOVE YOU to all the boys. A woman speaking to the public on the public ground at St. Mary's Gate told us to pray for tribulation in order that we might enter the Kingdom of Heaven and then set fire to herself and ran away down Deansgate screaming as the flames fanned by the wind turned her into a pillar of fire. These and all sorts of other things I remember but why I remember I don't know. Sometimes I think it is because I am frightened being here in this place and miles away from home but when I try to find a cause of being frightened I can't and begin to think that it is not fear I feel at all but something else. I know that when I was a baby and felt like this I cried and sucked my thumb or my mother's titties for comfort but now I am old and for comfort I don't know what to do. I lie awake in bed and listen to the noise of the nuns walking along the corridors up and down the stairs. Very light on their feet though they are, their long robes brushing against the floor as they move makes noise enough to deafen me, and then I think I hear them praying all the time morning noon and night for the souls of men. Maybe this is just imagination but ever since Sister Veronica told me that day on the beach that they are praying all the time for the souls of men, I've heard them at it. Last night I heard somebody crying and didn't know who it was. I stuffed the sheet into my ears and put the pillow over my head to shut the noise out but no go—

—I know now who is crying. It is Nina. I had a feeling it was when I first heard it but now I am sure. Last night she cried for hours and I just lay back and listened to her. She doesn't cry very dramatically. She makes hardly any sound at all. Am I the only one who hears her? Or does everybody else hear too and ignore it like I do myself?

—night she cried again. I listened for as long as I could bear it then I went to see her. I had to be careful leaving my room in case a prowling nun copped me roaming around at that late time of night. I opened Nina's door and went in. She was stretched out on the bed looking comfortable and fast asleep except that tears were pouring down her face. After looking at her for a long time and wondering what to do I decided to do nothing and left.

I have been given another book to read. Sister Veronica handed it to me and she looked apologetic. It is called *Dwell Deep* and written by Amy Le Fevre.

"What's this for, Sister?"

"Mother Superior told me to give it to you," she replied and read out to me the notice on the book's back cover: *"It will delight the girls with its well-conceived characters and its winsome though sometimes wayward young people—"*

"The Religious Tract Society?" I asked when she finished.

"Yes," she answered. "You're being brainwashed."

—Kitty Skidmore so they say has been in a children's home for care and protection. How these rumors get into this place I don't know. I think they crawl up through cracks in the floorboards. Kitty Skidmore has been in the Home for twelve months because of something her father did to her. The something is incest. When you ask the chief gossipers what incest is they think quickly and say: "O it's extreme cruelty. He burnt her with cigarette ends and beat her with the poker."

Only Nina and myself and Kitty Skidmore know what incest really is. If we told the other girls they'd faint—

—Kitty shivers all the time. Nobody likes her. Whenever she approaches a gang of girls talking they close their gaping mouths until she has gone by and then, as soon as her back is turned on them, they begin to laugh. She pretends not to care but she trembles and lets them

●

see it and they have no pity. One reason why they don't like her is because she gets special treatment. It isn't all that special really but these girls are petty-minded. Instead of Kitty getting washed with the rest of us in the big bathroom she goes to a private place and gets scrubbed and changed there—

—been moved into my bedroom. This is a shame because I like sleeping on my own but I suppose she's as much right to be where she is now as I have. It is no use asking her why she has come to sleep with me. She's telling nothing to nobody—

—like being in the company of a vampire or a nocturnal creature of some sort. She never sleeps. I only sleep a bit but compared to her I'm a dormouse. She lies flat out on her back on the bed with her hands folded on her stomach and her toes turned up to the roof. One of these nights while I sleep I think she might sink her fangs into my throat. I see the sheets moving as she trembles underneath them. If this goes on much longer I'll end up trembling too—

—the sun has started to show its face again. Yesterday was a beauty. We spent the whole time out in the garden or down on the beach. The sun being so bright gave Nina a good excuse for wearing her dark glasses. After dinner the little kids played on the swings and roundabouts but we older ones went wandering off—or at least Nina and I did. The others seem to like going around in

•

a group. At the back of the house there is an open space facing the sea. Soon, the nuns say, this space will be covered in thick juicy grass but at the moment it is covered in hard brown brittleness that must be last year's crop. We stretched ourselves out on top of it though, and lay there in the sun. It was very quiet. Every now and again we heard the sound of the kids on the seesaw in the playground. I turned my head to see if Nina was asleep but her sun-specs are so big and black that it is impossible to tell whether her eyes are wide open or shut tight.

"Are you asleep?" I asked her.

"Yes I am," she answered and took hold of my hand.

If anyone else had done that I'd most likely have told them not to but I let her go on holding it until the fat grinning nun came out into the garden and rang the bell for teatime—

—beginning of Lent. Everybody is giving up things for it. It is hard for me and for Nina too. We both know that the idea of Lent is to renounce something we enjoy so that we suffer until Easter Sunday.

"What are you going to renounce?" Nina asked.

"I don't know."

"And nor do I."

"I suppose we could give up food."

"The nuns wouldn't allow us to starve. We're here for the good of our health."

●

Sister Veronica who had been listening in inquired:

"Why are you so anxious to give something up for Lent?"

"We thought it was a rule."

"It's a rule only if you decide that you want to do it."

"It's hard to find something we enjoy enough to suffer without."

"There must be something you've got or do here that you enjoy."

"There's nothing here that I couldn't give up cheerfully."

"Then perhaps your stay here is a sacrifice of your happiness in itself," she said and moved away to eavesdrop on somebody else's conversation.

Out in the garden this morning I met the girl who does the weekly wash. I know she is very religious because she wears a golden crucifix on a chain around her neck, and a Saint Christopher medallion which she has had blessed by the Pope dangles from her watch strap.

"What are you giving up for Lent?" I asked her.

"O I'm not giving anything up this year. I'm going to put a little extra money into the collection box each week instead," she said and it was a good idea. If I had money I'd do the same.

—woman who has been asked by the Government to investigate children has arrived to investigate the children staying here. The Chief Nun told us that we are to answer truthfully all the questions she might ask us as her work will be of great benefit not only to us but to future generations.

"Sit down, my dear," the woman said when I went into her investigating room. "Now then I want you to write your name age and address at the top of this sheet of paper. Use my pen."

I did so.

"I want you to understand that everything we discuss here in this room will be strictly confidential. Your answers to my questions—"

Notice she didn't bother to ask me whether I wanted to answer her questions. O no.

"—are private. When the report we are compiling is published no names will be mentioned. You will be nothing more or less than a statistic. Understand?"

"Yes."

"Right. Question one. What sort of school do you attend?"

"An ordinary school."

"A state school?"

"Yes."

"Good."

"What's good about it?"

"Well, not so many years ago a girl of your class would not have received any education at all. From the cradle you would probably have been sent to the mill or the

•

factory. You'd never have known the glories and benefits of a good education. The present society we live in however has raised the standard of living of all classes to heights hitherto unheard of—undreamed of one hundred, nay, fifty years ago. You are a fortunate child indeed to have been born into a compassionate and enlightened age."

"O," I said.

"Have you taken the entrance examination for the high school?"

"Yes."

"Pass or fail?"

"Fail."

"Never mind. Nothing to be ashamed of. At a secondary school you will be receiving an education ideally suited to your capabilities."

"Yes."

"Good scholar?"

"Yes."

"Get good marks in exams?"

"Yes."

"So you'd say you are an intelligent person?"

"Yes."

"And a somewhat conceited one too if I may say so."

"You may say what you please."

She lit a cigarette and blew smoke in my face.

"I will. Don't worry. Religious family background?"

"Yes."

"You go to church?"

"Every day."

"How very commendable. Who was Moses?"

"The Prophet who led the Israelites out of bondage."

"Any trouble in the family? Divorce. Separation."

"My mother's been divorced twice and she's separated from her third husband."

"Broken families. The cause of more trouble—O well. Do you feel any bitterness about this?"

"Yes."

"Do you approve of divorce?"

"No."

"How right you are. Do you know the Ten Commandments?"

"Yes."

"Have you broken any of them?"

"A few."

"Which ones?"

"Thou shalt not steal."

"You've stolen?"

"Yes."

"What sort of things?"

"Only food. Because I was hungry because my mother never used to feed us. I had to steal or else me and my little brother would have died."

"Do the police know about this?"

"My mother was put in jail for cruelty and neglect."

"Not harsh enough. Have you received sex education at school?"

"Yes."

"Extensive?"

"Well—just the facts."

"Are you a virgin?"

We faced each other across the table.

"No," I said and hoped God wouldn't strike me dead on the spot for lying.

"Are you a virgin?" I asked.

"That is neither here nor there."

She wrote something down on her sheet of paper.

"You know this sort of behavior is wrong?"

"Yes."

"How many times has this sort of thing happened?"

"I don't know."

"Are your parents aware of this?"

"Don't know."

"Do many of your friends behave in this way with boys?"

"Don't know."

"You don't know much, do you?"

"No."

"Do you know the consequences of such behavior?"

"Yes."

"You don't care?"

"I don't know."

"Have you no moral fiber?"

"What's that?"

"Something you haven't got obviously. Good morning. And send the next girl in on your way out."

I left her and told Nina to go in.

"What is it?" she asked.

"Just a nosy Parker asking questions again. Tell her a pack of lies."

And Nina did and I hope everybody else did too just to give the poor old soul a thrill. I'm not kidding there's always somebody poking their nose in where it's not wanted. Your life's not your own any more—

—Passion Week Fever is mounting up. A giant-size statue of Jesus Christ Crucified stands in the garden. It has become an object of adoration. Every day girls and some nuns stand before it and sometimes deck it with flowers. I have looked at this statue of Jesus Christ on the Cross and can't say I'm in love with it. It is grotesque but grotesque in a small way. I don't know where it came from. I know where I'd like to send it. Many a time I feel like demolishing it but it's too big—it's smallest toe is longer and fatter than my leg and the wounds in the hands and feet and side are big enough for rooks to nest in when they get the chance. It is a monster statue and instead of making you feel agony at the agony of what it is trying to imitate it makes you feel agony for

●

yourself that you've got to look at it and agony for the man who made it that he should have been so untalented. The rooks' nest in the left-hand nail wound has been destroyed by the gardener and the other rooks spend all their time protesting about it at the tops of their voices—

—rehearsals for the special Passion Week church services. The choir which sounds like a cats' chorus at ordinary times sounds worse now that it has really got something to sing about. The choir members wear special blue frocks and white veils on their heads and are now trying to get special expressions for their faces. These special expressions are modeled on Sister Veronica's. She is very beautiful and always looks elevated and white and pure and gaunt. Everyone thinks she is the holiest of the holiest but I'm beginning to think it's just an act she puts on. Many a time she has behaved in an un-nunlike way and said a lot of un-nunlike things but always on the sly though, so that no one will start to think she is a falling angel. I only hope I am there when she does fall. I bet she does it with a smile on her face. The whole house reeks of church smells from top to bottom and turns my stomach over—

—girl is locked up in the sickroom. The doctor has given her drugs to keep her quiet. For the last couple of days she has been getting fiercer and fiercer in her devotion to Jesus and once or twice has told me that she has

●

seen visions of the Virgin. When she first told me this tale I thought she was joking but it's no joke. Not now. We were on the beach this morning enjoying ourselves in our various own ways when all of a sudden we heard a commotion and went to investigate. There was the girl on the ground. She writhed and moaned and there was blood on her face.

A gawping woman in the small crowd said: "Stigmata." And crossed herself.

Sister Veronica glared at her as much as to say: "You silly old cow." And she picked the girl up off the ground and carried her away toward the house while we followed on behind. A silent procession.

"Stigmata. What's that?" Nina said.

"Are you talking to me?"

"You're the know-all," she muttered darkly.

"Stigmata's when people start bleeding from their bodies when they haven't been cut or stabbed or anything. It's religious. Like some girls faint when they see their favorite film star."

"Like being sent?"

"Yes. I saw a woman once in church who fell to the ground and beat her head against the stone flags halfway through the service. It was very interesting. Two men carried her out and laid her on the grass verge of the cemetery, while we all went on inside singing our heads off not taking a blind bit of notice. Or at any rate we all pretended not to be noticing. Everybody's ears and eyes were twitching, to tell the truth. Nobody likes to miss anything. Not sensational things. Sister Veronica looks very majestical carrying that body over the sands, doesn't she?"

"Wonder what she thinks now?"

"She isn't allowed to think. Not think anything that might be against what she is, anyway. That'd be treason. If anybody found out she was thinking treason which is as bad as doing it really according to some people she'd be hanged drawn and quartered—and I'm sick of it all and I'm going away—"

Nina looked surprised when I galloped off away from her and the rest of the procession but she didn't follow me which was just as well because if she had've done I'd have gone mad. I couldn't stand the thought of going back to the Home, and decided to spend the rest of the day on the beach seeing what was cooking there to take my mind off my troubles which were all unidentifiable anyway but troubles all the same. Eastertime is a big holiday for most people and while it lasts they make the most of it. I watched a man set up on the edge of the retreating sea a Punch and Judy stall. Toby Dog with a white frilly ruff around his neck walked on his hind legs and barked for attention. People ran straight into the water and screamed and yelled as the first cold of it touched their bodies. A boy in blue trunks decorated

●

with badges gave a fine exhibition of swimming and at the end of it stood up in the water looking pleased with himself. I clapped. He bowed. A woman wearing a red scarf around her hair and an old leather pouch across her stomach led seven donkeys along the sands. Their reins and saddles were decorated with silver bells and brass studs. Seven donkeys named Marlene Daisy Winnie Monty Carmen Hope and Kitty.

"Sixpence a ride. Sixpence a ride on the donkeys."

The woman made the announcement and in no time at all was in business. All the kids on the beach wanted to take advantage of her offer and soon the donkeys were trotting to the breakwater and back—some trotted at least but one refused to exert herself and walked the set length ignoring all gee-ups and get-a-move-ons. Grown men too rode the donkeys and dead daft they looked doing it. Most of them had had a few beers and pretended to be cowboys and Indians chasing each other. O the donkeys stood it all but I'll swear they had a good laugh about it to themselves on the quiet. The Donkey Woman watched and sucked her bottom lip and turned the silver sixpences over in her money pouch. Gangs of old women walked down to the water's edge and tucked their skirts up and removed their shoes and stockings. They laughed until they cried when the cold water lapped over their corny old feet. Punch began to beat his Judy with a big stick. She screamed and hit him back.

●

All watchers shrieked and Toby Dog scratched a flea in his fur.

"I hope this excellent weather lasts," a man said and poured a frothy bottle of beer over his head for cooling purposes.

I was so engrossed watching his performance that I walked backwards and trampled down a Union-Jacked sand castle. The little lad who'd built it yelled and his mother shouted at me. I ran. Looking over my shoulder after putting a good distance between us all I was surprised to see what a small space the holiday-makers had crowded themselves into, in spite of the whole beach being wide open enough to give each person enough space to found a dynasty in. The sandhills are high in parts and tough grass grows on them. They are used a lot by lovers and Peeping Toms looking for thrills. I left the beach and walked along the nearest ridge but saw no one—no lovers, no Peeping Toms—no nothing at all. Not even a sea gull though I suppose they were about—probably they were cadging food off the holiday-makers. I walked a long way determined to reach the headland far away. I have often looked at the headland and fancied making a trip to it but the nuns say it is too far for us to walk. All of a sudden I heard thundering hooves and saw galloping along the sea-edge a donkey with a full-grown man on its back. The man looked scared stiff and kept shouting but all his whoas and stops and swearing made no difference to the donkey who pounded past as if it was running in the Derby or something. Then WHOA the man screamed and the donkey did as if he'd put the brake on. Over its head shot the man and landed thud on the hard sand. The donkey didn't stop to look at its fallen passenger; it just kicked its back legs in the air and then it shot off again toward the headland, while the man sat stupid on the beach and only moved when the sea broke over him.

Water waves I once was told are of two kinds: oscillation and translation. Waves of oscillation are the ordinary deep-water waves in which all the particles of water within the waves move in circular orbits. At the surface these orbits have a diameter equal to the height of the waves. They decrease rapidly with depth until at a depth equal to the length of the wave the movement is practically zero. In a wave of translation the whole body of water moves forward and does not return. Pay attention, said the teacher, and tell me what causes waves of the sea. Whenever the wind blows over water the surface is formed into waves. These grow under the influence of the wind, form an irregular surface pattern known as sea, please teacher, and when wind-raised waves travel out of a storm area they advance as swell but not all waves are caused by wind some are caused by earthquakes submarines landslides or volcanic eruptions sometimes known as tidal waves but true tidal waves are

●

caused by the sun and the moon but really teacher although waves have been observed for thousands of years knowledge of them is most incomplete and many fundamental questions remain unanswered. Thank you, child, sit down.

I had thought that the beach was deserted after I left my holiday-makers at the other end of it but as I reached the top of a sandhill I saw not far off a crowd of people making a lot of noise. I approached the crowd slyly and watched it for a long time. Some of the people in it were old and some were young kids but the more I looked the more I realized that they were all daft—or anyway daft in the way we think daft is. At home near us there is a special school for Mongol children and many a time I have seen these children playing out or going for walks. Some of them are very big—one looks about twenty years old but when I was six he looked about twenty years old. He's got a big head and a great loose mouth that seems made of rubber. And there he was on the beach with all the other children. They must have a Holiday Home here. One thing about them I noticed is that although some people are very scornful of them and often say that it would be better to kill them when they are born they don't look as miserable as some who think they are the cat's whiskers so to speak. I have often thought that a lunatic—so long as he or she wasn't the sort that does terrible atrocities like raping and bludgeoning—would be a better companion than the cat's whiskers sort. I liked watching them all playing on the beach—one little girl hadn't got any control over herself and couldn't catch the ball that was being thrown about. She got in a flaming temper about this and screamed. Nobody took any notice—I felt a bit jealous. Many a time I have felt like screaming myself but the only time I ever did I was treated as if there was something wrong with me—and maybe there was but what it was I didn't know—it just comes on me sometimes to scream but you're not allowed to let it out—if I screamed out loud every time I felt like it I'd be put in a home for mental defectives and a home for convalescents is bad enough. I wondered if the big lad from the Home near us would recognize me if I showed myself and when I did he waved and his rubber mouth turned up like a crescent moon in his face.

"Share our picnic," said the man in charge of the kids and I did.

"We're here for the day," the man said. "We have enjoyed ourselves."

I stayed with them until they decided to leave late afternoon and when they'd all gone I turned back home myself. It got dark and I missed the girls in their summer frocks and the lads in their shirt-sleeves and even the bashing-ups of Punch and Judy. The runaway donkey on his return journey caught up with me and walked behind me three paces. The tide turned and went out leaving the sand uncovered for miles wet and hard to walk on, but the sandhills were dry and seemed to be shifting but it was the wind blowing the fine sand about that's all and I was sorry because I'd like to see sometime the mountains move—a sight worth seeing like earthquakes and volcanoes. In a dip in the sandhills I came across a flock of sea gulls clustered round a man who was feeding them with bits of things. The man beckoned me. I lingered remembering a little girl I know who was lured down an air-raid shelter by a Lascar seaman off the docks who pulled her knickers down. She was saved by a woman who used to tip her rubbish in the shelter and came then and scared the sailor off. But the man beckoned again. I looked around and saw no one. The man waved a piece of chocolate at me. The girl I know was tempted by a piece of Yankee chewing gum. All the same I took the chocolate.

"What's your name?" the man said and threw a piece of cheese at a sea gull.

"Haven't got a name. Only a number. What's your name?"

"Same as my dad's."

"What's your dad's name?"

"Same as mine."

So we finished the silly game no wiser.

●

"You shouldn't talk to strange men."

"I know. My dad's warned me not to but I like chocolate. You've given it me, haven't you? You don't want paying for it?"

"No. I don't want paying for it. Not in same or in kind. Do you live around here?"

I put Nina's sunglasses on for protection. The sun had gone in but the moon's as good an excuse for wearing them as any.

"No. I don't. I'm staying at a home for sick children."

"Are you sick?"

"Don't I look it? Everybody says I do. Do you live here?"

"No. I'm in transit."

"Where you going?"

"I'm just having a long walk."

"Have you been to Scotland?"

"Yes."

"I like the sound of bagpipes."

"I knew a Scotsman once. A sergeant in the Black Watch. A bloody lunatic. One of the original Ladies from Hell all right he was. Won the V.C. for his valor."

"You've been a soldier, haven't you?"

"How can you tell?"

"You can always tell soldiers—demobbed ones any-way—my dad's got a demob suit just like the one you're wearing."

"Dirt cheap and nasty aye I know but never mind the clothes don't maketh the man."

"This chocolate's the sort sailors have, isn't it?"

"Yes—black and bitter. Would you like something sweeter?"

"No. I like it bitter and black like this."

He started to light a cigarette and all of a sudden he began to shake. First his hands. Then his shoulders. Then his arms and legs. A friend of my dad's suffers from the same trouble but once when we were out together and he started trembling all over a nosy woman said:

"How disgusting. Drunk at this time of day."

O you silly sod I almost said to her face but then I thought why bother it's not worth wasting breath on.

The man bit the end of his cigarette through as another shaking spasm got him. I lit the cigarette and stuck it in his mouth.

"Puff up," I said. "My mum says smoking does you no good—but puff up. You may as well."

And he took a long drag at the cigarette and seemed better for it.

"It's shell shock, isn't it?" I said.

"That's it."

"My dad's friend's got it. Much worse than you, though. He does it every ten minutes. I think he'll be doing it even after he's dead and buried. When they

71

put him in the cemetery it'll be like a molehill with the mole trying to get out. He'll never be still, I'm sure."

"No. And nor will I, I sometimes think."

"You never know. You're younger than him. He's old as the hills and ought never to have been a soldier according to his wife but he insisted. I wouldn't have done. I'd have run away, sooner than be a soldier. I can't kill a fly without feeling guilty about it and soldiers are for killing all the time, aren't they?"

"Or defense."

"Well, whatever they're for I wouldn't be one. They only make men soldiers anyway so I'll never be made to be one. Will I?"

"I hope not though they do say your sex is the deadliest one."

"Do they?"

"Aye. They do."

"I'm not saying I wouldn't fight if I had something to fight about—I'm always fighting anyway about something and I suppose a war's got to be fought by someone —but I hope I never have to do it—I mean I'm not saying I'd let someone walk over me, I wouldn't but—O you know what I mean. I always think it's a bit daft the way they make people go and kill each other—still—I suppose it's all because people are daft to start with or else they wouldn't do it— Do you think they like killing each other or something?"

●

"Some do and some don't."
"Did you?"
"No."
"But you did."
"I did."
"Well then."
"Well then. That's it. My dad did it too. My mother's still got a letter that the priest wrote to my father while he was at the last war— O said the priest in this letter to my father, O my son keep your soul and your sword clean, one for the Glory of Your Father In Heaven and the other for the Turk. And my father did. And you know they have no pity for us such men of learning and sensitivity. O no. Some do and some don't, I said to you, and did you you said to me. I did I said back I did. I did. In my ignorance and my innocence. And some laugh some scorn while others merely wonder I do not laugh or scorn and need not wonder I know, though you stand withdrawn from me I cannot withdraw from you not of my own free will or want of trying I have and now retreat out of sullen misery into rioting despair that shrieks and howls and tears me tooth and nail and my yearning does yield Implacable it scorns consolation. I'd better be going now—come on I'll see you home back to your Home for Sickly Children or whatever it is you're in—keep your soul and your sword clean, my Daughter—

●

one for the glory of God and one for yourself . . . come on kid . . . get moving . . ."

We walked back to the Home and Sister Veronica standing at the gate said nothing when he left me there but led me into the house and upstairs to my room and said nothing and on my own I lay in bed and lay with my ear against the pillow and listened and felt the sound of my own heart beating and held my breath in case it stopped and I dreamt of birds so beautiful so beautiful so beautiful upon the grass . . .

Tom
Riley

Tom Riley

There is the sound of children playing in the streets and the barking of McCluskie's dark brown dog—tied to the leg of the kitchen table in order to preserve the virtue of the pedigree bitch round the corner who anticipates a worthier lover.

On top of his ladder the window cleaner whistles and shakes his hips to the rhythm; then leans back, pleased at the sight of his own reflection in the polished glass.

Tom Riley on his mother's instructions counts carefully the sacks of coal as the coal merchant empties them down into her cellar. This particular dealer is notorious for giving short measure if he thinks he can get away with it, and you've got to be careful.

The tall man twirls his red mustache and knocks on Emmie Carter's front door (*Personal Service Guaranteed*, the notice says in the newsagent's shop window). Emmie opens it, they smile and Tom just has time to see the red mustache quiver with delight before the door closes behind them both.

Four sacks of Grade III delivered, the coalman straightened his back, daubed black dust on Tom's white face, then boarded his lorry, driving it out of the boy's sight; and Tom relaxed once more amongst his shawls and cushions, his hand-knitted socks and scarves, to proceed with his reading—page one, *The Boy's Book of Modern Marvels*.

Tom Riley was a delicate child—his mother insisted on it. There had been a time when Tom had wondered what all the fuss was about. A time when he had looked and felt exactly like any other small boy; but as his mother continued to protect him from toothaches and bellyaches, from broken heads and bloody knees, and particularly from other children, he had come to realize that he was indeed worthy of all the attention he received and never failed to marvel at the wonder of himself.

School had finished for the day and the local heroes were gathering together. They had their company headquarters in an air-raid shelter down at the bottom of

•

Nashville Street, and many a time Tom had tried to join this band of mighty warriors and cunning hunters, but at his approach . . .

"Here's Tommy Tin-ribs."

And the chant would go up . . .

"Tommy had a thick ear,
Tommy had an ache,
His daddy tied him in a sack
And threw him in the lake.
His Mam went for the doctor,
But the doctor wouldn't come
Because he had a pimple on his bum, bum, bum!"

And Tom would retreat, adopting a policy of aloof indifference. "If I don't look at them they won't look at me."

But they did. And they would come pursuing him like furies. Standing on the other side of the street, jeering their nonsense songs, performing their insulting pantomime, until the enraged appearance of Tom's mother, flying to her son's defense like an avenging angel, scattered them far and wide, daring them to return. And they did return. They could run faster than the woman, and should Tom ever decide to stick up for himself, then they felt quite capable of dealing with him.

Sometimes they did ignore him, but even then he

found little or no peace—caught between relief that they were leaving him alone and curiosity as to what they were going to do next. They got up to all sorts of tricks and always they were in trouble. Such trouble that the neighbors would shake their heads and wag their tongues, and Tom's mother would thank God that her son knew better; while Tom longed to be condemned beside the renegades, strutting, swaggering and swearing with the best of them, flirting with the long-haired girl next door, escorting her on mysterious errands down back entries after church on Sundays, playing wag from school, giving cheek to his teachers, to his mother, to everybody. Resplendent in his imagination, he would sit on the front doorstep, pathetic in his reality, engrossed in the adventures of other children, watching the street, listening to his mother move about the house, waiting for her to fill him up from head to foot with every conceivable kind of remedy for every conceivable ailment; and at such times Tom remembered his grandfather.

Tom had always been fond of his granddad. He was a rare old man and as kind as anyone could be. He worked in the mill, on the handlooms, for his living, from six in the morning till six at night, and as soon as his day's work was done he'd make tracks for home, swinging the heavy clogs on his feet, steady and slow. All the children used to love him and they'd wait for his coming every night, because they knew his pockets would be filled with toffees and apples or something just as sweet and just as good for them to eat.

Every evening, as soon as the kitchen was sided up, the pots and pans scoured out and stacked away, the old man spread out on the table before him an assortment of paint pots, glue, pieces of string, bits of wood, hammer, nails and pliers, and fashioned from these fantastic toys for his grandchild. He sang over his work. Told tales and made such fun that it seemed then, as it still did, that there could never be a better way of passing the time; and Tom never went to bed till the last song had been sung and the last tale was told.

One Sunday last summer Tom and his granddad had gone to the Lake District. The weather was fine, the air fresh, and they walked for miles, the old man as tall and straight as a Maypole, for he'd been a soldier and still carried himself like one. They stopped and ate on the lakeside at Coniston and the Tom who wolfed down salmon-paste sandwiches, cold pie, cherry cake and brandy snaps was a very different Tom from the boy at home who fiddled with his food till it got cold and had to be thrown away.

It was very warm in the Lake District last year and as they sprawled in the grass in the heat of summer, the old man telling tales about his army days, Tom saw a poppy bud open up into a most beautiful flower and watched a butterfly on the branch of a tree struggle from its chrysalis, twitch for a minute in the sunshine, then fly away.

The return journey had been long, and Tom fell asleep on the lap of a woman in the railway carriage while his grandfather entertained his fellow passengers with numerous excerpts from *The Messiah,* and the woman, moved by the great work and the well-oiled voice, heaved in her seat, her chest rising and expanding with such emotion—smothering Tom's head in warm and ample flesh—that her breasts grew bigger and rounder every moment, like two smooth silk-skinned balloons, and it seemed that they must explode.

On leaving the train Tom swapped the soft and billowing bosom for a perch on his granddad's stiff shoulder. The buses had stopped running for the night, and it was a long walk home. The old man put Tom to bed, and as Tom looked up at his grandfather's face, a face with so much of the angel about it already, he got quite worried and feared the old man would be leaving him soon. And the boy was right.

His grandfather worked up to the day of his dying, going so quickly that Tom scarcely had time to notice, being sent from the house to stay with his Aunt Bella till the funeral was over; and when he returned to his home, there was little to indicate that his granddad had ever lived there, save for the toy-making tools in the cardboard box under the sink and the clogs.

And now a lodger occupied the old man's room. A quick and furtive fellow, sliding in and out of the house on wheels, with his coat collar turned up above his eyes, his hat brim pulled low over his nose, like a fugitive from justice, kicking the cat when he thought no one was looking.

But Tom in bed at night and dreaming could still hear his grandfather. He would listen for the sound of the old man approaching the house, swinging the heavy clogs on his feet, steady and slow, striking sparks from the pavement and beating out such a rhythm on the earth that the whole city seemed to shake and rattle. Sometimes he entered Tom's bedroom—by way of the chimney. And he would stand there on the hearthrug holding his two sides and roaring with laughter at the commotion he'd caused, until Tom joined in, and the pair of them would howl with glee together again.

The children were singing again. Christmas was coming and they had discovered that each season brings its own rewards. The Christmas Carol Campaign had been set in motion by The Brains of the organization, a slim-necked boy, his face chubby with adolescent sensuality and marked with the fundamental characteristics of the rich and influential gangster of the future. Having plotted these maneuvers, The Brains was sitting back in the air-raid shelter, awaiting the return of his satellites who had been launched throughout the city with instructions to strike swift! strike hard! And no one was safe, not even Tom. For The Brains saw in Tom's pale and sickly appearance unlimited scope for exploitation: a picture of Tiny Tim in *The Child's Illustrated Dickens* had suggested to him that Tom, equipped with a wooden crutch and a temporary limp, would be a useful recruit to the ranks of his troupe.

But Tom wasn't interested, or at least his mother wouldn't allow him to be; so The Brains, having risen to power mainly on the frailties of others, discovered Tom's weakness and set to work on it.

Tom had always wanted a bike, a red one preferably. But his mother wouldn't allow it. It seemed that many years ago when she first rode a bicycle a most distressing accident had occurred and she realized that the same fate would inevitably overtake her son if she ever allowed him contact with a similar machine.

So The Brains acquired a bike, and a red one it was too. He rode it up, down and round the street, ringing the chromium-plated bell, steering it with his feet, hands in pockets, until Tom driven nearly mad with envy consented to defy his mother and struck a bargain.

Tom was to make two personal appearances weekly with the carol singers in return for which services he was

•

given temporary ownership of the red bike; this was kept under lock and key in the air-raid shelter where Tom could sit and look at it to his heart's content.

Tuesdays and Fridays after school, instead of going to the public library and spending an hour's instructive browsing there, he met up with his colleagues and they set out together in search of a few spare and easy coppers. Things were going very well. So far they hadn't knocked on the same door twice, realizing that familiarity breeds contempt, and an efficient routine had been worked out. Procedure as follows: push Tom to the front of the group, makeshift wooden crutch and cocoa tin collecting box carried before him like some holy sacrament, then knock on any door. As soon as it opened, question:

"May we sing you some carols, please?"

Should the answer be No, then they would go elsewhere, having wasted no time on an unprofitable venture.

And Tom was happy. But his mother wasn't so pleased, seeing her son's bright face as yet another symptom of the strange and unidentified disease that plagued him. He didn't any more play with his food till it got cold; instead, down it went like fuel into a furnace keeping the ovens hot and the energy at boiling point, as Tom hurtled through his life catching up with himself at last. No more the dreary drag to school each morning and the mad dash home as if pursued each night. Up early—tired to bed. And Tom sang in the streets with his dark angels . . .

> *"Christmas is coming,*
> *The geese are getting fat,*
> *Please put a penny in the old man's hat.*
> *If you haven't got a penny*
> *A ha'penny will do;*
> *If you haven't got a ha'penny*
> *You're a skinny old Jew . . ."*

And fled for his life down to the sly river that runs through the middle of the city.

A long time ago, in summer, boys used to swim here naked but not now. The Littlebrick River is hidden under a thick piecrust of factory refuse and the water can hardly be seen. It's a good hiding place, though, for runaways and outlaws, marauding Indians, sought-after criminals, and especially for impertinent carol singers who find their seasonal employment MOST PROFITABLE.

The money poured into the cocoa tin and every night The Brains, murmuring "Good work, boys," pocketed the lot until a few days before Christmas when, after the big share-out, Tom, with a handful of silver sixpences, found his services no longer required by the carolers. He was on his own again. The Brains had returned the red bike to its owner and had confiscated the wooden crutch

●

—twirling it high above his head like a drum major as he led his company of merry men through the city on one great and glorious shopping spree—leaving Tom to follow at a safe distance.

Every store and shop and market stall received a visit from the spendthrift boys—jewelers' shops and toffee shops—tobacconists and toyshops—until, money all gone, they found their way back to the river, and The Brains beckoned Tom closer. . . .

"D'you want this for Christmas, spindleshanks?"

The crutch. As Tom reached out for it, The Brains threw it down into the river. . . .

"If you want it, get it, sparrowlegs."

And the boys, intoxicated with their prosperity, rushed Tom off his feet, then stood still, gaping and amazed as he drifted down into the water disappearing beneath the whipped-cream snowdrifts of scum.

Then run the Merry Men frightened at what they've done while Tom weeps in the water, too shocked to scream for help, and soon too tired to fight as the Little-brick River pushes him down and down still further. . . .

There are no children playing in the street this Christmas morning and McCluskie's dark brown dog isn't barking. The tall man forgets to twirl his red mustache as he knocks on Emmie Carter's front door and she forgets to smile as she opens it. Tom's Aunt Bella comforts his mother in the back kitchen, and a half-dressed Christmas tree stands in a tub near the window. Upstairs the cupboards are crammed with secret presents for the dead boy—and the whole street mourns.

The
Teacher

mystery person wrote on the school wall—

> *O Mr. Slovve we thee implore*
> *To go away and sin no more*

Mr. Slovve did go away—the only trouble was he kept coming back. Officially he came back because of the teacher shortage but in our opinion he came back because he liked the going so much—and he was never known to say No to the present we had to buy for him at the end of the school year.

"We are assembled here," the headmistress would say

once we were all settled in the big hall; "we are assembled here to say good-bye. The end of the school year is always a mixture of sadness and joy. Joy because we can all look forward to six weeks of summer holiday; sad because we must say farewell to some of our dear friends who are leaving us for pastures new. We have a great tradition of teaching at this school—we seek here not only to educate the mind but also to educate the soul. We teach you the pleasure of physical exercise—the team spirit of games too, for when you leave school finally you will find that life is a game, sometimes serious sometimes fun, but a game that must be played with true team spirit—there is no room for the outsider in life. One for all and all for one. Here we try to teach you that work need not be something to endure but a joy. We try to instill in you all, the pride of achievement. A job well done, whether that job is high or lowly. But I won't go on. We are all anxious to start our well-earned rest and no one here today will deny that Mr. Slovve, our own dear Mr. Slovve, has earned his rest. As you all know he is retiring from the teaching profession today. He has been teaching for many years. Hundreds of children have passed through his hands and not one of them would deny that his influence on their lives has been all for the good. Mr. Slovve, we have bought you a small retirement gift. Every child and teacher in the school has contributed towards it. When you look at it we hope

●

you will be happily reminded of the many days you have spent here with us."

The gift would be presented to him—O how many gifts he had—amid applause. He was very moved. And one or two terms later he would be back.

At one point during his many retirements he got married and the headmistress sent him an invitation to the school Nativity play. We were anxious to see his wife. When we did see her our anxiety changed to puzzlement for Mrs. Slovve was a girl and though Mr. Slovve was tall and slim with a straight back he was well over sixty-five and his hair was white. True enough his cheeks were rosy red but they were very old cheeks all the same. And then there was the matter of his glass eye. But these things apart there was something about Mr. Slovve that repelled us all. We didn't know what it was—it wasn't his methods of teaching though they were bad enough. He would enter the classroom and we'd jump to our feet chorusing "Good morning, sir." "Sit down," he'd order and "get your books out. We've a lot of work to get through." His lessons consisted entirely of note-taking. He had everything he wanted to say written down in a black book and he'd dictate to us at top speed. No time for questions—anyone who wanted to ask a question was quelled with a glare from that glass eye. That eye would have turned the tide it was such a terrible dead eye.

"I hope you got all that down," he'd say when the

lesson ended. "I want you to learn those notes off by heart. I want you to get good marks in the examinations. And you especially had better have the notes down correctly." Then turning to me, "I want no more funny business from you, you long streak of nothing. And don't look at me, you sullen child."

Mr. Slovve was very fond of making jokes about his pupils—especially the pupils who had some special physical characteristic. I was the tallest child in the school, so I was the "long streak of nothing." Richard Sheridan was the smallest child in the school—he stammered too and also squinted. You can imagine what fun Mr. Slovve had with him. He would always begin by asking Richard how he was getting on with his speech lessons and Richard who was gentleness itself and without malice would start to tell him clearly and without trace of his stutter, but the more he spoke the bigger the smile on Mr. Slovve's face grew and in the end his smile would reduce Richard to his usual silence and all his lessons counted for nothing. People always say that children are cruel but there was only one child in the class who laughed when Mr. Slovve made fun of me or Richard and that child was a boy called Harold and Harold was Mr. Slovve's pet so he had to laugh whether he felt like it or not out of loyalty.

Harold had been Mr. Slovve's favorite since we had all been in the infants' school and over the years their affection for each other became intense. Mr. Slovve lived in a big house surrounded by a garden and in the garden grew apple trees and pear trees and Mr. Slovve brought bags of their fruit to school for his pet and sometimes he would bring a bunch of flowers for Harold to give to his mother. One Christmas he brought the lad an expensive fountain pen—which seemed a waste because Harold was so thick-headed he couldn't write properly. At Easter-time he would be presented with a big chocolate egg with HAROLD written across it in yellow icing sugar. While we couldn't understand what Mrs. Slovve saw in Mr. Slovve we couldn't understand what Mr. Slovve saw in Harold for Harold was the color and texture of porridge.

"He looks as if he's made out of plasticine," I told my mother once.

"He can't help the way he looks. Maybe he's got a disease," she'd say. "Maybe he was born like that just as you were born tall and Richard was born small."

During our last year at that school when we were all approaching our tenth or eleventh birthdays Mr. Slovve's fancy for Harold became embarrassing. The teacher stopped reading his lessons from his book and instead set us to read them ourselves so that while we were all busy he could summon Harold from his seat and have the boy stand beside him while he sat at his desk. Mr. Slovve's desk was very big. We used to watch

●

their activities from the eyes in the top of our heads and wonder what the teacher and his pupil were murmuring to each other. And then Richard, who for all his squinty eyes could see better than any of us, enlightened our innocence. At first we discussed the matter but gradually our interest dwindled away into uneasy silence. We'd all been told about the dangers of taking sweets from strangers. We'd all heard and read about child-murders—one of our schoolmates had been found naked and strangled to death in an old air-raid shelter. But we kept silent. And Harold got good marks for his lessons and his pockets always jangled with the silver sixpences that Mr. Slovve gave to him.

Christmas came round and the school Nativity play went into rehearsal. Because I was the tallest child in the school, I had always been given the part of the Angel Gabriel. I had special silver wings made for me and a special golden halo. I was never all that keen to play Gabriel or to play anything else for that matter but orders are orders—until Mr. Shovve changed them. He decided that Harold should play the Angel. It seemed a pity because whatever else I might have been I was prettier than Harold and the thought of a porridge plasticine Gabriel didn't go down like a good dinner. But Mr. Slovve was convinced.

"After all," he said, "the Angel was of the male sex so why have a girl playing it."

●

This seemed reasonable enough but he couldn't leave it at that.

"And especially why should we have this girl playing an angel? With her silent brooding way of looking and her atrocious accent. Why don't you have elocution lessons, girl? Improve your speech. You're living in England—why, only God knows—you should at least speak the King's English correctly. You children make me despair. You'll amount to nothing. You come from the gutter and that's where you'll stay if you don't make an effort to cultivate nicer manners and nicer ways. You're rough. I'm telling you this for your own good. If you want to make a better life for yourselves than the life your parents have had it'll require effort. You can't expect us to do everything for you. I know the class most of you come from. It's a stubborn society. Old habits die hard. The Government takes you out of the slums you were born into and it puts you into new clean houses and what happens—they go to rack and ruin—they're dirty and squalid—any money that comes into the house goes on cigarettes, fish and chips and the cinema—you keep the coal in the bath—"

"Coal in the bath," I said to myself. "That's a funny place to keep the coal."

"What are you whispering about?"

"I'm not whispering, sir. I'm talking."

●

"And might we know what you were talking about?"

"Coal in the bath. It seems a funny place to keep it. I never knew anybody who kept it there."

"As you get older you obnoxious creature you will discover that you don't know everything. Personally I believe that your state of abysmal ignorance will be permanent but hope springs eternal even in me."

"Yes, sir."

"And now, children. I will announce the rest of the Nativity play cast list. Richard Sheridan will take the part of Joseph."

"But Joseph has to make long speeches," poor Richard stammered.

"I know that, Richard. And I intend to make his speeches even longer. You must learn to live with your defects."

O yes. Richard did learn to live with his defects. In front of a large audience of mothers and fathers and relatives he doggedly made his tortuous way through the part, his undersized body swathed in striped blankets, his oversize head lolling beneath the genuine sheik's headdress—a trophy of Mr. Slovve's service in the Camel Corps—he was made to wear. At one point I calculated that it took him three minutes to say *There is no room at the inn, Mary*. The audience driven most unwillingly to distraction twisted and squirmed in its seat. Angel Gabriel smiled. Mr. Slovve's rosy cheeks burned rosier.

And then it was over. And Richard sought vengeance. And Richard had vengeance.

Mr. Slovve retired for good and without speeches without glory without gifts. Richard was the only one who cried. He had no pride of achievement.

My Uncle, the Spy

My Uncle, the Spy

$\mathcal{M}$y uncle was a spy. He'd been a spy for twenty years. He did not try to hide the fact. He did no other work. Whenever anybody asked him what his profession was he'd smile and say "I am a secret agent."

One night he sighed deeply: "I'm getting old. Tired. I think it is time for me to retire."

The thought of my uncle retiring from his job amazed me. He was so glad and so proud to be a spy.

"A man can't go on forever. The day thou gavest me Lord is ending. I know that. I'll just quietly disappear. And the work isn't what it was. It's an overcrowded profession. Become fashionable. There aren't enough secrets to go round any more. Some spies are having to invent secrets in order to earn a living. Otherwise they would starve and their families too. And then there's automation. I know more about automation than most people and we won't ever escape it. It's invincible. I can't help wondering what will happen when redundant spies join the ranks of the unemployed."

"Where will you disappear to, Uncle?"

"O there are places. I've always hankered after a warm mild climate. Not too hot. Not too cold."

"But where, Uncle?"

He looked secretive.

"Is it a hidden place like the burial grounds of the elephants?"

"I'll send you a postcard."

"When will you disappear, Uncle?"

"Soon."

The postcard was delivered by hand. It bore no sourceful postage stamp or postmark. *I am well* my uncle had written upon it. His disappearance, sudden and mysterious, grieved his relatives greatly. They told the police and they inserted a photograph of him in the *Missing from Home* column in the *News of the World—*

Pavan
for
a Dead Prince

Pavan for a Dead Prince

A death while bringing sorrow and sometimes joy brought something else with it when I was a child—sightseers. It was customary then—and still is—for friends, relations and any other interested parties to visit the bodies of the dear departed before the burning, burying or embalming took place. Most people only bothered to view for the last time corpses of people they had known well in life but some were not so particular and went to see anyone's corpse whether known to them or not in life. One woman who called herself my mother's friend though my mother despised her and never pretended not to, had this dead-watching down to a fine art. Every night she would go through the Death Columns in the

●

newspaper with a fine-tooth comb making note of any
lately deceased persons who sounded interesting enough
to merit a trip:

"Frederick Corny—aged ninety-five—a great age that
is—Maria Moravia—aged six years—God rest her soul—a
baby—sounds foreign to mmmm . . ."

Into the pages of a small red book she would copy
their names and addresses and later on, suitably composed, would go to their homes and ask to see. Her
request was rarely, if ever, refused.

This visitor was always showing this anxious interest
in death. When I was little I used to think it was a good-
luck token to see a dead body like touching a sailor's
collar or seeing a pin and picking it up but as I got older
I realized it was a hobby, always received reservedly in
our house. She talked while my mother worked and my
father read.

"A child. That's all she was. A baby. She looked
beautiful. I'll swear she wasn't dead. Catholic family.
Candles all round the coffin. Her cheeks were so rosy and
her lips were so red."

And my father would wink at me and my mother
would spit on the iron. The spit hissed at the iron's heat
and bounced off it like lead shot.

He left school when he was fourteen years old and
went to work with his father down the mines. Every

night the pair of them came home from the pit together covered in coal dust. Every speck of it had to be washed away before they were allowed to set foot inside their house. Stripped right down to the waist—out in the backyard in all kinds of weather—they'd pour buckets of water over each other until the dirt disappeared. By the time Benjamin had finished scrubbing himself he shone. He was a big lad to start with and the longer he heaved the coal the bigger he became. He wasn't big in the style of muscle-bound apemen who go in for dynamic tension and take part in this year's Adonis or Mr. Universe contests. The power of his body was elegant and graceful and subtle. Girls fell for him left right and center. They wolf-whistled him on the street. They'd line up and wait while he took his pick. They wrote him love letters which small boys delivered by hand, thereby earning themselves a penny or sometimes a sixpence depending on the pressure of the passion involved. Whenever he took a girl out it was a foregone conclusion that they would go dancing. He loved to dance. To watch him dance and to dance with him was a treat.

On a Saturday night in a mild September he took me to see a troupe of performing Spanish Gipsies who had turned up all of a sudden at the local bughut under the auspices of an organization bent on bringing a bit of culture to the working classes. We eyed the poster pasted outside the theatre. *Genuine Spanish Gipsies* it said. We

looked at each other and then back to the poster.
Conchita. José. Maria. Yerma. We looked at the photo-
graphs. Neither of us objected strongly to somebody
assuming that we came from a class short on culture but
to be considered brainless into the bargain was, we felt,
in bad taste. But we paid our money and we took
our chance. As soon as those Genuine Spanish Gipsies
pranced onto the stage all our suspicions solidified.
There wasn't a pinprick's worth of Spanish blood between the lot of them. I have Spanish blood in my own
veins—a bit watered down now since the day my great-
grandmother blew in from Barcelona on the arm of my
great-grandfather, a seafaring gentleman from this fair
city—and it can always detect itself in others. We didn't
hold the deception against them however. The company
consisted of a small tight man with hair like a distraught
steel-wool panscrub, a tall thin woman, a short medium-
weight woman, a large stout woman and a boy who
played a guitar when he was not trying to beat it to
death. The tall woman was a grotesque clown who
arched her back and ground her teeth together, the short
woman's performance was memorable for the way she
flashed her large mouthful of snow-white china choppers
about in the spotlight, the fat woman hammered her
way from one corner of the stage to the other, holding
her skirts high above her tree-trunk legs with one hand
while tinkling tiny golden bells attached to the finger-

tips of the other, the man—taut sinister and dramatic in black—twitted bulls, fought duels, tamed wild horses and wild women, polished off glasses of wine and tossed his head so enthusiastically it was a wonder it didn't fly off its handle. Although we had never seen such dancing before it didn't take a professor to tell us that it wasn't a very good exhibition we were watching. We had the time of our lives though. Probably because the dancers enjoyed themselves so much. The audience cheered sometimes booed catcalled and made rude remarks but the dancers did not mind and gave as good as they got. At the end of the show the small man was transported and danced the soles off his leather boots in his ecstasy. We clapped him up until our hands were red raw and went to bed that night well satisfied for once with our dose of culture.

We lived in the same street in houses that faced each other head on. All the houses in the street, whether they were on the right-hand side where the sun shone or on the left-hand side that was always in shadow, were identical. Two rooms up two rooms down no bathroom no garden and one backyard each. My bedroom and Benjamin's bedroom were directly opposite and sometimes if we did not draw the curtains we could see each other in bed and many a time we talked to each other through our windows across the narrow street. When I was getting ready for bed one night I looked across into Benjamin's room. What was he doing? At first I thought he was having a bad attack of Saint Vitus's dance but I watched and wondered for a while longer and then it suddenly struck me. All that hip wriggling, heel stamping, hand clapping and head tossing. He was working out a Spanish dance routine. I kept him secretly under observation for a long time and night after night he kept at it. He was dedicated. It was very interesting. I never mentioned anything to him about his gipsy dancing and he never mentioned it to me.

At Eastertime he got rheumatic fever. He went into the hospital and stayed there for months. In due course he came home and I went to see him. All the shine had gone off him. There isn't much you can say to somebody you love who has been very ill. You can tell them how sorry you are that they have been sick. You can tell them how much you have missed them while they've been away. You can tell them how much you would miss them if they went away for good. You can wish them well soon but somehow the words that come out of poor mouths at such times never sound anything like what you wanted them to so I said nothing. The fever had weakened Benjamin's heart and he wasn't allowed to do anything strenuous for fear of overstraining it. For weeks he had to stay in his bed which his father had brought downstairs and pushed up against the window so that he could see what was going on in the street. He saw all sorts of things through that window. How much of it was true and how much of it he made up because he was bored I don't know but he told me a lot and I always felt that I knew everybody's business better than they knew it themselves. Some people said it was a mistake for me to see him as often as I did, maintaining that my presence did him more harm than good. Maybe it did. I don't know. I wouldn't go and sit with him when other people were visiting. They always got on my nerves with their pity. I suppose it was pitiful that Benjamin had to lie around all day instead of being on the go but he didn't need reminding of it all the time.

"You'll soon be on your feet again, son."

"Doctors don't know nothing. Especially the National Health Service Wallahs. You'll be cutting a rug at Madame Jones's Ballroom with the rest of them this time next year," they would jovially say.

Looking at them I used to think that they were the pitiful ones in actual fact with their horrible hypocrite hope. The trouble with me was that I had had no practice in visiting the sick. The small refinements of sickroom procedure escaped me. I would be ushered into the presence of my pale and pajama'd lover, his bowl of fruit, jug of orange juice and the smell of disinfectant as chaperon; my intentions were always honorable. I started off those evenings all sweetness patience and good nature but it was ten to one that before very long our tempers, which matched each other step for step for violence, quickness and complete unreasonableness, would smash the peace up into blazing quarrels. And I would get myself gone bearing all the blame. And then if it wasn't a ferocious and remorseless argument that got the invalid dangerously worked up it would be too much laughing that caused the trouble. Everything had to be extreme with that boy. I'd say something funny and before either of us knew where we were we'd be rolling about holding our stomachs and wiping tears of laughter from our eyes. Reproachful looks from his mother would drive me away. O you can't win, I said it then and I say it now.

The day came when he was allowed to leave his bed. At last. He was thrilled to bits. He had gone very thin. I held one of his hands up to the light once because I felt sure it would be transparent. His face was white and his eyes seemed bent on burrowing their way out through the back of his head. He was allowed to walk round the park twice a day.

"Big thrill," he said when told.

The park was very small and very barren. The trees were encrusted with the filth that passes for fresh air in all industrial cities. A valiant grass covered the ground like a threadbare carpet. Fiendish flower thieves and murderers disguised as tiny children and little old ladies

●

stalked the city gardens. Twice a day round this he went as quickly as his legs could carry him for he hated the place. There were better places but far away and he wasn't allowed to make the journey. His mining days had gone for good, the doctor said, and his dancing days were over too. He was fed up.

"You'll have to do something else, that's all," I said to him one night.

"Such as what?" he asked.

"Such as stopping sulking just for five minutes."

"You'd sulk worse than me if you were in my place."

"I know I would. Are you going to spend the rest of your life sitting here in idleness and misery?"

"Yes."

"Well, so long as you don't expect me to sit here with you it's all right."

"I thought you loved me."

"I do."

"You don't show it."

"What would you like me to do?"

"Comfort me in my trouble. Treat me nice. I'm delicate."

"I'll comfort you with a big hard brick one of these days. Right in your left eye. You could read books."

"I don't like reading."

"You could paint."

"I can't paint."

"Why don't you take up knitting and sewing then?"

"And you go down the mines digging coal."

"You're not taking me seriously."

"O I am."

He loathed his weak heart. He would stand with his hand on his breast reciting carefully and with feeling every swear word he knew: "Fucking heart bleeding heart buggered heart sodded heart . . ."

We were walking home from the pictures one night after seeing a good film about an internationally famous ravishingly beautiful female concert pianist who discovered she was dying of T.B. when he invited me to an exhibition of Spanish flamenco dancing in his bedroom.

"And who's going to flamenco?" I wondered.

"Ferdinando Jones here."

"You'll be reclining in a small plot of land in Saint James's Church of England Cemetery if you're not careful," I told him.

"I know I will," he said and hopped skipped and jumped along a hopscotch chart that a child had chalked out on the pavement. "But there's one dance left in the old man yet you know."

The exhibition was an event cloaked in necessary mystery. He had to give it when his parents were out of the house. If they had discovered his intentions they would have gone mad. I was sworn to secrecy and promised on my mother's life not to tell a single soul. On the night in

●

question he led me by the hand up to his bedroom. He draped a thick dark heavy army blanket over the window to spite nosy Parkers who were always on the peep. He stopped up all cracks and spaces in walls and door where sound was likely to get through. He set his gramophone in motion.

"I hope this build-up's justified, Benjamin."

"It'll be something you'll remember all your life. It'll be the high spot of your existence and mine too."

At first he made jokes about himself but the more engrossed he became in what he was doing the less self-conscious he was about doing it. He was completely absorbed. He danced like a demon. He danced for all he was worth, generating a radiance around himself. I got drunk on the sound of the guitar and the sight of him. His face shone and I felt again the incredible fierce frightening desire for something beautiful that we had shared with each other. Then it stopped. We stared at each other. We glared at each other. We hated each other then like deadly enemies. He lost his breath. Falling across the bed he lay still on it and stared at the ceiling through wide-open eyes. It occurred to me without fear or surprise that he was going to die. Whether he would die there and then I didn't know and that didn't matter. He would die. I put my hand over his thundering heart and placed my mouth against the pulse in his throat and watched the ritual beginning.

•

"Not years." He had got his breath back and was able to speak. "Not years."

"Do you think I'm daft?" he asked me.

"Why?"

"For dancing like that?"

"Why should you be daft?"

"Did I look funny?"

"Do you care?"

"No."

"You didn't look funny. You looked lovely."

"If anyone found out I liked that sort of dancing they'd think I was a fool."

"Only people who think that anything they aren't interested in and know nothing about is stupid and useless."

"Before I was ill I'd been practicing. It was after seeing them fake Spaniards that night. Do you remember? I enjoyed watching them. I like dancing that way. Means more. Doesn't it? Don't you think so? You can put more feeling into a flamenco than you can put into a foxtrot I'm telling you."

The Procession formed up. Quiet men and women—sightseers feigning sorrow to conceal curiosity—all bowed grave and dignified and moved into the cere-

●

monial. Doffed caps. Wet eyes. Deepest sympathy. Silence. Whispers—

    —a tragic

    —a young lad like that

    —good die young

    —his poor mother

    —what a waste.

But his face had shone again.

    "What's funny, kid?"

    "Nothing."

All About
and to a
Female Artist

All About and to a Female Artist

She has writing talent but it is too untamed as yet to stand up and take a theatre audience by the throat. . . .

It is probably fair to say that it is one of the best plays ever written by a nineteen-year-old photographer's assistant. But coming from anyone else my reactions would not be nearly so benign . . . she knows as much about adult behaviour as she does about elephants. . . .

Sex—but it won't pay. . . .

Structurally the play is a shambles. . . .

●

We met outside the theatre on the first night and deplored the whole thing. . . .

A sophisticated West End audience was apparently fascinated like students of insect life looking under a rock for the first time. . . .

Broadway has bought the play—does only sordid stuff sell now . . . ?

It is an unhappy thing that a young girl of 20 years should have such a low thought pattern. . . .

DEAR MISS DELANEY,

I do MOST SINCERELY hope that you forgive so great a LIBERTY in writing this humble LETTER to you like this.

Again I beg of you to forgive me as you don't know me I know. But I am so ill with worrying I feel I shall have a nervous BREAKDOWN and END UP in a mental home as I can feel my BRAIN snapping. So as a last resort I've taken this GREAT LIBERTY in writing to you and expressing myself. So PLEASE, Miss Delaney, don't be annoyed at me will you? As I could scream and run away honest I could this place is driving me MAD. So quiet at night always and I'll never forget this unhappy Christmas, hardly anything to eat much and no music to help things. Because a few days earlier to Christmas I had to pay my rent arrears up. My poor children couldn't understand it. No presents hardly. No music. Please God may this year be a little different for me, as I don't think I could take any more trouble. I do hope you will kindly read my HUMBLE letter and understand it. But first of all may I wish you every success in all your future. No doubt you have been poor and had many troubles but may Almighty God guide you in your future years. Well now I will write and explain myself. I hope I won't bore you because you will have experienced sorrow sickness and being hard-up yourself. So dear Miss Delaney PLEASE I BEG OF YOU DON'T TELL A SOUL OF MY LETTER TO YOU. PLEASE DO TREAT IT WITH EVERY CONFIDENCE. But I must tell someone as my inside is aching and my heart is about broke already because the past year has been so long AND BITTER towards me as I've known like yourself sickness bereavements and lack of money. Everything that could possibly happen has happened to me. Also in the early part of last year I got a wireless and television all in one. £64 it was to buy it. Well I got a part-time job to pay for it but as I've had eight children I suffer from very varicosed legs and every now and again one breaks out on my ankle into an ulcer. WELL, it broke out again and I had to give up my job and to crown all this I was going into town one day trying to

●

get a cheap piece of meat for the Sunday's dinner and Dear Miss Delaney I went into Woolworths Shop to get a reel of cotton and I lost my purse with everything I had inside. Well I was in tears outside the fruit market and asked nearly everybody about it till I couldn't stand any more. So I set off home walking and this meant I had to borrow some more money till the next week and that's how it went on until I got all SNOWBALLED with debts and so on.

Dear Miss Delaney and now being so in a fix like this my wireless and television is CUT OFF and the H.P. payments are due on it. It is so very miserable as I love music and plays too. I'm so absorbed in plays and never get tired of listening to them or watching them. By the way I did not mention but I am a Roman Catholic I don't know if you might be but I've sent you this little picture of Lourdes as it's a special year ending in February. I'd have given anything to have gone to Lourdes but I'll always be there in my humble prayers to Our Blessed Lady. So I do hope you will keep this picture Miss Delaney and pardon my awful writing as my nerves are so bad with worry. I'd give the world to have a clear mind and my music on again as it does help to make life bearable. Don't you think so? Music seems to soothe one's nerves and just now it being so quiet in my house it would help me a lot to have some but it has all been cut off on account of the payments being overdue. I do hope I have not bored you writing like this but I have simply told you my troubles as a friend and I hope you will be kind and read and understand the letter of a humble and honest Catholic mother down on HER LUCK BUT HOPING for BETTER DAYS IN STORE. Please God they will come soon before I crack up as I can feel it coming. Also I have just put all my kiddies to bed—it's only 5:30 but as it's school tomorrow I have to wash and dry their clothes. So I'm waiting for the fire to burn up and I'm finishing this letter to you and posting it this evening but as it is snowing outside I am not all that anxious to go out as I have only got poor velvet ballerina slippers to wear. . . .

DEAR SHELAGH,

I do hope with all sincerity you won't mind my writing to you and asking a very big favour. You see it is like this. I've decided to write a very good play and it is taken from true facts—in fact it will make a very good film I am sure. I seem gifted for this sort of thing but have not known how to go about it. I've also composed three songs just one after the other. The play I have in mind could even be left to me to direct. I could even act the part I've that much confidence in it. I'd just like to give up working damned hard for a living in any case. It is not my life at all. I love the Theatre.

●

DEAR SHELAGH,

As I have not had a reply to my last letter to you
I thought the letter might have been misplaced and I
did not know your proper address. I have a daughter
your age and we have both found life very difficult of
late. She did not make a happy marriage having married
on the rebound. There is nothing wrong with him except that he is not one to get on. My husband and I
lived in England till some time ago where he was in
business. Then after the war the young men returning
to civilian life threw him out of his position and we
never seem to have recovered ourselves for this reason—
we have always kept elderly relations from both sides of
the family. They dreaded going into homes or institu-
tions and so we kept them and in each case they died
peacefully with us. My husband keeps going but only
just. He is such a brick and so plucky but he is a lot
older than me—nearly 70—and it is not fair for him to
have to take on the jobs he takes at his age. I made up my
mind last year that if we went on like this I would not
have him much longer and so I started writing. I have an
uncle a journalist and an aunt a novelist so I feel I
might be able to do a little this way. I have known a lot
of theatricals from time to time as I once had an uncle
who was a theatre doctor and I worked as his nurse and
saw a lot behind the scenes. So you can see how des-
perately anxious I am to have this play of mine taken on.

●

If I could only get it bought for the films my troubles would be lessened if not over for our needs for the future are not like those of a young person like yourself. I think you must be extraordinarily clever and your success well deserved. Success spoils some people. I know it will not spoil you. You are the true Lancashire type as my husband is from the same place originally. God bless you and if I am not lucky I must carry on and not complain. I hate to write this letter as—please believe me—I am not a scrounger who wants a star to help them I am sickened by what I read about people who do that sort of thing. All this is leading to this—can you—and I mean will you—lend me £100? One thing is this—you must believe in me whatever happens. I am a Methodist Minister's daughter brought up in a good home so you are dealing with a conscientious decent honourable person. You must believe this. I would never rest until every penny had been repaid. You may say "have I no friends I can ask to lend me the money?" You must understand dear that when one comes down in the world one is very independent and does not mix much and make friends. That is why I am asking you for this favour as you are cut off from my life here and no one need know about it as I am very sensitive about it indeed. That is why I ask you NEVER to MENTION THIS TO ANYBODY AT ALL. If you can lend me the £100 will you send it to me Monday or Tuesday (registered in notes if possible or a money

order which I can change easily). I'll acknowledge at
once and then arrange with you accordingly. I'd like no
one else to know at all as it is a thing I hate doing. I'd
be deeply grateful as you can imagine. I am afraid this
letter might sound presumptuous and rude which is the
last thing I want to appear. If you help me now in my
need I will not forget you but will include you if I have
any success with my writing. As I said before my daughter is very unhappy in her marriage and I would like
her and her husband to be living nearer to us and would
also like to set them up in a small shop if possible. Also
my son has recently come out of a sanatorium and is not
yet strong enough to take a job and with my husband
also being ill—but such a brick—the brunt of the work
falls on me and if things don't get better soon it means I
will have to take a job and that is why I am hoping that
the play I have written will be a success. It must be nice
now that you are a success to be able to take care of your
loved ones. God bless you, my dear, and I would like a
reply as soon as conveniently possible. . . . Yours in
anticipation.

I would like to know if you would let me write to
you as a pen friend. I am thirty years old and play the
harmonica. I have won two or three talent contests playing the harmonica . . .

●

So it seems that London audiences not only enjoy their dustbin atmosphere outside the theatre but inside it as well. How are you all sinking? I am an Australian. What a disgrace not only to the name of THEATRE but to womanhood you are with your dirty clothes and grubby skin and hair. Aren't you ashamed of yourself— I trust at least that your new affluence will enable you to buy a bar of soap. By the way how are your Teddy boy boyfriends. Do they carry flick knives? It would be rather fun if they jab their flick knives into you one night it might teach you to improve your tastes and company—

ANONYMOUS

Your play has been misunderstood by all the theatre critics and all my friends. Let me explain it. It is not about sexual fulfilment but a rest from sex and states that such a rest can only be temporary . . . seen thus the play has a theme development and a form. I suppose this is new to you too? . . .

It has long been my desire to write to you as I think you are a writer of genius. Being an Eastern artist myself your play is pregnant with a valid symbolism which will automatically adjust itself as time passes. I am 23. My work has been described by top British critics as "miraculous" "best" "elegant" and "inspired" . . .

●

No doubt you will be surprised to receive a letter from North Africa but I have been intending to write to you for a long time so here goes. I am interested in writing myself and have written a play. It is a thriller type and has an Australian background and an original plot plenty of action and suspense. Further, before I continue, I may say that I come from the same part of the world as yourself—Lancashire. Now back to this play I have done. It has the mark of a good play and will also be suitable for a film and T.V. Should you be interested in acting as my agent for this play then I will give you 20% of all profits and later you can help me with another play I have in mind. I would also like to have you as a pen-friend and can promise you some very interesting letters . . .

Shelagh
Shelagh delaney
hellllooooooooooooooo

and so the weather goes in this a'way and out that a'way . . . ooooo . . how merry oooo . . . let me sing . . . let me sing the song of weather . . . and in unison . . . one and two and three and round and round the weather goes and where the weather stops

●

no one knows
you in your small house
shall there be commerce between us
you who are on the way up
and I in the whirlwind
following the 360 degree path of life
going all ways
shall there be commerce between us

karma

FRED

Vodka and Small Pieces of Gold

Vodka and Small Pieces of Gold

*W*ord's got round that I am going to Poland. I have been pulled up many a time by the nosy ones in the streets of this city. The nosiest of the nosiest —a woman—stopped me this morning on Broad Street. This woman always has plenty to say but she never says anything unless it's already been said by somebody else. With her it's always "my husband maintains" or "according to the *Daily Express*" or "a man on television was saying last night," and never *I say* or *I think*.

"My son says you're going abroad. That right?"

"Yes."

"Where're you going?"

"Poland."

She started to lift the topsoil of her memory digging deep for something about Poland that her husband, the *Daily Express* or a man on television might have planted there some time or other.

"Wasn't it Poland caused the last war? Yes. It was, you know. My husband always maintained we should have let Hitler have Poland if he wanted her. According to him she was neither use nor ornament to anyone. He was always keen on the Germans—always said Hitler had some good ideas especially about Jews and niggers and the Communists. He fought though. Lancashire Fusiliers. The army changed him. What are you going to Poland for?"

"I've been invited there."

"If you want a holiday you ought to go somewhere you can have a good time."

"Why shouldn't I have a good time in Poland?"

"They're all Communists there. You want to be careful. They might let you in the country but there's no guaranteeing they'll let you out again. They'll do anything to further their own ends. Look at all these eggs they're sending over here?"

"Eggs?"

"Red eggs. They're very cheap. A lot cheaper than our eggs. That way they hope to undermine the English egg industry according to my husband. A typical Communist trick he says. They're very sly. He won't allow me to buy any of them. He says he's not having our money going over there to build more H-bombs."

"O," I said.

"They're not Christian over there either. Anyone who believes in God gets persecuted."

As it happened we were standing outside one of the dozens of old churches in the city now converted into warehouses. I refrained from commenting on this and merely observed that Poland is a Catholic country.

"Rubbish!" she exclaimed. "Rubbish!"

"Rubbish or not it's a fact."

"You kids might believe propaganda as my husband says but you can't expect old dogs like us to be taken in by it. We've seen too much. I've lived through two world wars, you know."

"I know. All the same Poland's a Catholic country."

"The police carry guns there."

"The police carry guns in America."

"They're not Communists though. Mind you my husband's no patience with the Yanks either—he can't stand them. Not at any price. Look at all this trouble in Berlin. My husband says that if the Americans had any sense they wouldn't waste time arguing with the Russians over Berlin. They've got the weapons, he maintains, so why not use them? Just show the Russians who's boss and they'll soon start behaving themselves. I mean what happened last week when the American Vice-President

●

went to Berlin? He looked at the wall and all he did was distribute ballpoint pens inscribed with his name to the natives. What good does that do? You can't blame the Russians for thinking they're dealing with a bunch of big babies, can you? The Russians, according to my husband, only appreciate force—look at all these nuclear tests they're going in for. These nuclear tests have terrible effects on us, you know—they cause deformed children and all this leukemia. They pollute the milk we drink and if they pollute the milk they must do something horrible to the food. It's criminal. They ought to be stopped. I'm glad to see the Yanks are starting testing again—that'll show the Russians."

"American nuclear tests are just as dangerous to us as the Russian tests."

"But at least they're on our side as my husband says. Are you flying to Poland?"

"Yes."

"How much will that cost you?"

"Don't know yet. I haven't found out."

"Be expensive. Still, I suppose you can afford it. My husband says you must have a nice little bank balance by now. He was calculating how much income tax you must pay. He maintains you must be in the supertax bracket by now. You ought to go to the South of France for six months. I would!"

"I've been to the South of France."

●

"Italy then."

"I've been there too," I told her, praying God wouldn't strike me dead on the spot for lying.

"O well," she snarled through her dazzling white china choppers, "you've just been bloody well ruined, haven't you?" and covering herself in sudden busyness, "I can't stand here all day talking to you. Some of us have to work for a living. I'll have to write a play, won't I? Then I can retire as well," and she pushed off.

—It was always my ambition to travel on the Orient Express as I have always thought I'd make a good female spy but alas the Orient Express is no more—

—without my glasses in Poland! A disaster. I can manage to walk around without them but I don't see things clearly—everything comes to me through a mist. O well. I'll just have to make do with the poor eyesight God saw fit to give me—

—Poles seem to be as much condemned to a diet of caviar, vodka and the Polka as the English are to rare old port and pheasant. I don't see anyone walking about in chains and the Polish police look to me as sinister as the police do anywhere else. What about the Secret Police? They're keeping themselves secret—and what makes you so sure that that man behind you in the dole line isn't something big in MI5 and how do you know that your chambermaid at the Waldorf Astoria isn't the Mata

Hari of the FBI? O you can laugh. Mind you I don't think anyone could be blamed for thinking that Warsaw is the headquarters of an international spy ring because every third person you see wears dark glasses, smokes heavily scented cigarettes through amber holders and carries a pigskin briefcase—

—Writers Union House in Warsaw where I am staying (but not for long I hope) overlooks Zamcowy Square which is the spittin' image of Trafalgar Square, being full of pigeon-courting tourists and tourist-courting pigeons who smooch with each other while the cameras go off left right and center.

"The column in the middle of the Square was erected in 1644 by Wladyslaw IV to the memory of his father King Zigizmund the Third."

I stopped to listen to the guide addressing a group of German ladies.

"It is the work of the court architect Constantino Tencalla and the sculptor Clemente Molli. The Germans hewed the column down in 1944. The King's statue, though damaged, escaped destruction and when we embarked on our rebuilding after the war the column was re-erected in the Square which is the entrance into Old Warsaw."

This Old Warsaw proves once again that appearances are deceptive for it is only a reproduction of Old Warsaw not the real thing. Like the pigeons in Zamcowy

Square who cause King Zigizmund a lot of bother I have few feelings for history but Old Warsaw impresses me. I admire the thoroughness with which each building— each church, each shop, each house—had been reconstructed from old plans and old pictures but I am probably more impressed by the things which are not so easily seen. Some Poles and some visitors to Poland say that it was foolish to reconstruct a whole area as it was hundreds of years ago until the Germans destroyed it. They might say that it would have been better to take the opportunity of building a modern, more convenient place, but just as our ancient monuments act as physical proof of our long existence so this Old Warsaw does for Poles; and apart from anything else, to entirely rebuild something that has been deliberately and systematically destroyed by an enemy exactly as it was, is the sort of gesture that should be made now and again—

—never good at catching taxis. I always feel foolish when, after making a public exhibition of myself by calling waving and whistling in the street the thing sails past me. Like this afternoon. In the end a taxi stopped beside me and as I was explaining where I wanted to go to the driver, in my broken Polish, a woman nipped smartly out of a shop and sat herself down on the back seat.

"Excuse me," I said, "but this taxi is mine."

"Where do you want to go to, young lady?"

"The Central Park of Culture."

"O that's not far," she said, "take a bus instead."

The taxi moved off and I watched it out of sight. Warsaw like every other city in the world has its rush hour and this was it. I waited for a tram. If you can travel on a Warsaw tram in the Warsaw rush hour and still retain friendly feelings toward Poland, then it's a sure sign that your intentions are honorable. Tram travelers seem to be under the impression that the Polish trams are bottomless topless and sideless. People pile into them. Once it has been certified that every possible space inside the vehicle has been filled, the assault on the outside begins —soldiers children priests nuns businessmen, hunters back from the woods with their dead rabbits and pigeons, dangle from the steps and cling to the windows while the Polish winter weather belts through them. It is a good idea all the same to travel on the outside of the tram—otherwise, if you are crushed inside, you are likely to miss your stop and find yourself traveling backwards and forwards on the route like a prisoner undergoing a peculiar punishment. I endure this punishment daily. Once, as I clutched a strap, a heavy man fell against me. His hair was white. His coat had an astrakhan collar. He smelled of vodka.

"They ought to sell these things for scrap iron," I muttered subversively to myself in English.

●

"There are taxis, you know, young lady," the man said.

"I know there are," I said and tried to edge away from his intimacy. His left arm circled my shoulder. His head fell gracefully onto my breast.

"You're not holding the strap correctly," he said. "I could tell you the correct way of holding it but I won't. Not now. Not since female emancipation. You're not a Polish girl."

"No. I'm English."

A Kansas City scream rent the air.

"O you're speaking my language."

"Excuse me, madame," I said, feeling nasty, "but I think you're trying to speak mine."

Exerting all my strength I thrust the man away from me and hopped off the bus leaving the Kansas City Lady to herself. I found myself in an immense square dominated by a piece of concrete confectionery with red lights attached to its extremities. I had seen these red lights before and thought that they must be a new constellation. But alas! No new stars for me. The red lights are part of the PALACE OF CULTURE—a Russian gift to the people of Poland. This Palace has close family connections with the Empire State Building in New York. Whatever else you might think of these erections you can't help admitting one thing—they're BIG. The Palace of Culture contains 3,300 halls and rooms which can accommodate about 12,000 people. The cubature of the edifice amounts to 800,000 cu.m. and it is 230 cu.m. high. Inside there are theatres cinemas exhibition halls coffee bars restaurants a post office and a magnificently equipped youth club. Polish people are very tactful about it. It's a funny thing with Americans and Russians. They have a lot in common. They both want to be loved and cannot understand why certain parties prefer to keep the relationship purely platonic—"Go so far sir and keep your hands to yourself!" It isn't such a long way from Mack in New York buying himself a tie decorated with a handpainted nude female to Ivan in Moscow buying himself a tie decorated with a picture of a Culture Palace. It just goes to show what happens when culture gets too big for its boots— "But never fear, my dear," the old man said to his wife, "we've got Bingo." And that's a fact—

—"But whatever you do, don't rub it with anything rough."

—"O I've been using Brillo pads on mine for years."

—"The worst thing you can do. That's what he told me anyway."

"Well it hasn't damaged mine. It's in lovely condition."

The elegant English ladies stir and sip their tea in the Warsaw coffee shop. Coffee shops in Warsaw seem to serve Poles as pubs serve us—the only difference being the merchandise which consists of coffee teacakes and fruit juices. I have only come across one place—and that in the Old City—where you can sit and have a glass of wine vodka or beer in the company of friends and acquaintances. All other hard drinking as far as I can make out goes on behind locked doors though I have often seen, late at night, men standing in doorways drinking cheap vodka straight from the bottle as if it was water. True enough there are bars but these are in the bigger hotels. They are expensive places and cater to rich tourists and rich residents—the rich tourists are plentiful but the rich residents are not.

"This lack of inns does not affect the vodka sales however," my English-speaking Polish friend observed. "As a matter of fact the large number of alcoholics in Poland causes the government alarm."

"There you are," one tea-drinking lady said. "That's what Communism does for you."

"Yes," her companion answered. "Drives you to drink."

—Vistula Stompers playing in a students' jazz club located twenty feet underground in the dark dank musty rusty pipe-lined cellars of an old house. Jazz Caves—

"Why don't you take your overcoat off in this warm room?" I asked him. "You'll expire. And please sit down. You're hovering. You look lost. Like a refugee."

●

SWEETLY SINGS THE DONKEY

"I come from a long line of refugees," he said.

"Is that why you never seem to come to stay but always appear to be in transit?"

"That's it. The habits of a lifetime are hard to break off. They're national habits, though. I am not special. Just before you arrived here we feared war would break out over Berlin and the shops were stripped by housewives getting in provisions. When the war scare passed over they all had to queue up again to sell their large stocks of butter and sugar and tea back to the shops. There was a heavy demand for salt too. Some of the women had heard that salt rubbed into the limbs prevents radiation burns. Whether this is a scientific fact I do not know but salt was scarcer here for two weeks than water is in the desert. I tuned into a *Voice of America* broadcast round about that time and they were telling us how poor we are here and how we suffer from food shortage. It was very funny. My mother's cellar and cupboards were stuffed with provisions. Any stranger would have taken us for gluttons. My mother also considered changing all her money—which any good refugee knows is all but useless, what with different currencies and values—into small gold pieces and bits of jewelry and vodka. In time of war these things are the best currency. Their value is international. Our currency according to some people is a figment of our imagination. Once in Sweden I was introduced to a man from Western Germany—he would not shake hands with me—naturally this broke my heart—because he said Poland doesn't exist. As I said before, the habits of a lifetime are hard to break." He removed his coat sat down stretched his long thin legs out and lit his pipe—but all in transit—

—KOMIS! What does it mean? A lot of shops bear this sign. Look in the window. See some special Polish products? Marks & Spencer sweaters—Burberrys—Freeman Hardy and Willis shoes—Italian neckties—French kid gloves—American shirts—Swedish spoons? What's all this? An international jumble sale? Of a kind, yes. Foreign luxury goods are not imported into Poland in great quantities, consequently foreign goods are much sought after—to show a *made in London New York* or *Paris* label in your coat is as much a sign of your exquisite taste and wealth in Poland as it is anywhere else apparently. But not enough of these things get into the country, so what to do? Well—if Mrs. Parandowski has friends or relatives living abroad and they want to do her a favor like swelling her income (for most incomes here are small) they send her a parcel full of clothes—a dress, a petticoat, stockings and so forth—and then the KOMIS shop steps in, for these shops buy the foreign goods—and they pay well for them—from Mrs. Parandowski and then display them in the window at immense prices. Immense prices or not the goods sell and sometimes a woman will spend twice as much on a pair of English nylons as she would on a pair of Polish nylons ignoring the fact that Polish nylons are just as good as alien ones. It just goes to show, doesn't it—people are daft wherever they are and whatever they vote. Although Poland is regarded by many as the America of the socialist communist or-whatever-you-call-them countries there is a hankering in it for the lushness of Europe and the United States. This is natural enough, I suppose, but when they get twenty different brands of washing powder and baking powder in their shops all of ultra-super powers they'll probably start hankering for the simple time when washing powder was washing powder. In a café one afternoon I looked down at the peas on my plate. It suddenly struck me that they had no identity. English peas lead public lives. Every detail concerning their upbringing is made known. We know whether they are garden peas, frozen peas or processed peas—

—evening at the Warsaw Philharmonic with the dazzling audience promenading in the interval, heads inclining left and right, good evening how are you very well and you how nice to see you have you seen yes isn't she looking well—

—undomesticated aircraft bound for Cracow. Bitter weather. Passengers for Cracow line up alongside the plane. Names are called. All present and correct, sir! Permission to board given. That door closed with a quick self-satisfied snap. We're up in the air. No messing about here with fasten your safety belts please. Everyone laughs nervously and we all fall down as the plane goes up. It's getting hot. Everybody starts to sweat and strip. Which direction are we heading in I wonder? A conference up front elects a spokesman to have a word with the captain. He approaches the captain's door. He knocks. He knocks again. No answer. Maybe no one is home? But yes. The pilot hears the delegate and smiles and flicks a switch. The temperature is falling.

"This man is too ambitious," the shivering uniformed policeman in front says. The captain pokes his head around the door.

"It's raining in Cracow," he tells us—

—bus from Cracow to Zacopane. Well taken care of on the long journey by the other passengers who feed me with apples and biscuits saying:

"Angelskie?"

"Tak. Polskie?"

"Tak. Stanislaw."

"Shelagh."

"Christina."

"Shelagh."

"Tadeous."

"Shelagh."

"Kazimiez."

"Shelagh."

●

"Frederic."

"Shelagh."

"André."

"Shelagh."

"Josef."

A marathon of beaming smiles and shaking hands and a sad disbanding at the Zacopane terminus wishing one another good luck in all things always.

So here I am in the Tatra mountains millions of miles high and munificent with their beauty. I've never seen mountains like these before. O I've seen the Cumberland ones but compared to these they're tiny—but no less beautiful and to each his own when all's said and done. Now is the autumn. Only the tall pine forests stay green but the sun still shines. It seems a Polish autumn is warmer than an English summer so grab the sun while you can but relinquish it without bad temper when the early nights set in and admire the sleeping knight mountain called Giewont behind the black forest—are there grizzly bears and wolves in the forest? I wonder. No, they say, and smile. But there are bears and wolves and wild pigs too and the Polish Eagle, minus his royal crown now, wings it all over the place in wood and brass, sometimes bearing a painted madonna on his breast. The summer season is finished. The winter season won't begin until December. After Christmas the snow comes. Even so, Zacopane is still crowded with tourists and holiday-makers who come here for their health the air and the peace and wherever the tourists go the souvenir-sellers are. The people who live on the mountains are called *gurals.* —Very early one morning I walked along a track that led toward a group of wooden houses. In a field I saw a man and a woman. While the woman held the sheep's head the man was very thoroughly removing the animal's woolly coat with a pair of nail scissors. Recalling films about Australian shepherds who can shear a sheep with electric clippers in a matter of seconds, I watched the man working with nail scissors attentively—for me it was like seeing somebody roasting an ox on a spit over an open fire. The man spoke to me in Polish.

"I don't understand. I'm English."

"Oooooo—English," he said. "I speak English. American English. I was with American army in the war. Are you from Australia?"

"England."

"I would like to know more about sheep farming in Australia. They are all shepherds in Australia. How many sheep do they keep?"

"In the whole country?"

"Yes."

"Millions I should think."

"Tell me about sheep-farming conditions there—"

I was saved in the nick of time by the sudden appearance of a tall man who spoke to the shepherd in Polish.

●

The more he spoke the wider the grin on the shepherd's face grew. The man sat down on the grass beside me. He was very very tall.

"You're English," he told me.

"And you're American. You look like a cowboy I've seen in hundreds of Western films."

"That's me. I'm making a film over here."

"In Polish?"

"I speak Polish. You saw me speaking to these two. They laugh because the Polish I speak I learned from my parents who left Poland years and years ago. It's an interesting film I'm working on—it's about three American sailors of Polish descent who come back to Poland on leave. Some of it's wild. You live in London?"

"Sometimes."

"I love London. You know Simpson's? I buy beautiful cashmere sweaters there. It's odd, isn't it—you meeting an American cowboy in the Tatra mountains—"

"I suppose it is," I said. It didn't strike me as odd I must admit—

—outside Lenin Museum in Poronin. Couldn't go in because I had spent all my money elsewhere. A man and woman left the museum, talking:

"And in Egypt, you know, the people are so poor that you hire a man with a whip to beat the beggars off. I want to go."

●

—*Morskie oko* means the eye of the sea and the beautiful lake called Morskie Oko lies at the bottom of a basin one thousand, three hundred and ninety-three meters up in the Tatras. Only one house stands on the lakeshore— a big wooden house serving as hotel café post office and mountain rescue. The lake is almost a perfect oval. A mountain rescue boy took me by the hand, led me down to a boat and proceeded to row me across the lake to the far side where we left the boat and started to climb. The sun was shining, but still the way seemed bleak and seemed bleaker as we climbed higher. He led me through a narrow pass between rocks and gigantic boulders and we were on the side of another lake—the Black Lake. O if ever a lake lurked this one does. Three sides of it lap against sheer mountain walls which plunge straight down into the water. These walls are so high that the sun for most of the time is shut out or heavily shadowed. If Morskie Oko down below is the Eye of the Sea then surely the Black Lake up above is its brains—

—Suddenly the mountain wind has started to blow. It's early I'm told. Usually it comes to blow the thawing snow away but there is no snow so it blows and moans about the place like something lost and I feel sad and don't know why I feel sad.

"Ah," says a friend from the house. "It sometimes happens like that to some people in this place. Autumn is

●

always a sad time—especially here where there are so many sanatoriums for the sick the old and the dying—"

"Are you trying to cheer me up?"

"A glass or two of vodka will cheer you up," he said.

It didn't. I have heard people say that they drink to forget their sorrows but the more I drink the more sorrows I collect—

—Go back to Warsaw now and on to England then. I caught the Warsaw Express but only by the skin of my teeth.

"Ah!" said a starched black-and-white nun whom I had seen many a time in Zacopane. "Ah, you'll be late for the gates of Heaven one of these days, child."

It was a long journey. A young soldier who, from the look of him, had come straight off a battlefield, rested his long-haired head on my shoulder, stretched his legs, covered in crumpled khaki and dirty leather kneeboots, out in front of him and went straight away to the land of Nod. The nun, Sister Gertrude, opened *Perry Mason and the Case of the Mythical Monkey* and the policeman sitting next to her—gun holster and all—took his cap off, polished the silver Polish Eagle emblem on it and placed it up on the rack out of harm's way. He sat down and folded his arms. An old gentleman and his old wife faced me. The old man read the *New Yorker,* the old woman did a bit of knitting but after a while the knitting seemed to bore her. She put it to one side and rummaged around in her knitting bag. What was she after? We were all dying to find out. We watched on the sly out of the corner of an eye. She found what she had been looking for and placed it to mouth. A mouth organ? At the first blast the soldier woke up with a jerk. She played a few bars of Brahms' "Lullaby" and he dropped off again. Her husband closed his *New Yorker* and listened. She played the mouth organ very well. The Polish bobby said something. She smiled and nodded, and "Mack the Knife" came through next. Joyfully the policeman sang. Happy at last. After making his thanks he went off vocally satisfied to smoke contentedly in the corridor.

"I hope you do not mind that my wife is playing her mouth organ?"

The old man was worried.

"No. I don't mind."

He wasn't sure whether I meant it or not.

"She loves music."

His wife interrupted a suck to chip in:

"O yes, always I have loved good music. As a small child my father sent me to violin lessons but they were too expensive. I had to sell my violin. But I could not live without making music so I bought a mouth organ."

"Good idea."

"It is small and cheap. And good music is good music after all. A poor instrument becomes famous if the mu-

sician's heart is in the right place. In your country you
have the bagpipes?"

"In Scotland."

"I have been interested in the bagpipes. I would very
much like to play them. You see, I am ambitious."

She tootled on. Her husband smiled.

"Perhaps you are hungry, young miss?"

He opened a basket. Sausages ham cheese cakes biscuits—a bottle of Jugoslavian wine. It was a feast. We
made the most of it. The man and his wife had been on
holiday in Zacopane and were now returning home to
Warsaw. They had taught themselves to speak English.
The old man told me he was a waiter.

"An ancient waiter now but still a good one. I practice an ancient art. The art of being good waiter is not
known these days. It is despised. The young do not care.
Ah! They know nothing. The things I have seen."

The wine was doing its stuff all right.

"So many funny things have happened. So many sad
things too. And so many things to be regretted. Opportunities missed, O such opportunities. Once when I was
very young waiter, very handsome very conscientious, I
worked in a fine hotel in Warsaw. One day a famous and
very beautiful international female spy came to stay at
the hotel. One night she asked for a meal to be served in
her room. And I was to serve it. A beautiful woman.
Famous. My thoughts and feelings were unimaginable. I

took the meal—exquisitely prepared—and knocked on the door of her suite. She called me to come in. I opened the door. I went in. She was lying upon her couch—she was completely naked."

"And what did you do then?"

His eyes filled with bitter tears.

"I served the meal. Saying nothing—except perhaps, A little more wine, madame? And when the meal was finished I cleared the dishes away and said good night."

"Oh."

"A sad story?" he asked.

"From your point of view a tragic story."

The nun giggled.

"And now you are going back to England, young miss?" the old man asked.

"Yes, I am."

"You have chosen freedom then."

"Yes, that's it."

England in December. Christmas coming and commerce getting fat. It was nice to be back.

"Have you been brainwashed?"

"Yes."

"I see you have a bottle of vodka here. That's a sly piece of Communist indoctrination."

"It's for you."

"Thanks. What's it like in Poland?"

●

"It's not Utopia but no one pretends that it is."

We walked along and stopped at a bookstall. One shelf was crammed with newly imported American horror comics with titles like *Men, Action, Excitement, Climax.* I flicked through the pages of *Combat.*

"I won't rest until I see a goddam Red dangling from every lamppost in Moscow," were the words in the bubble coming out of the American hero's mouth as he marched off to the Third World War. I started to itch. Maybe this is the beginning of bacteriological warfare, I thought. I read on. The American hero was screaming at his wife, "They couldn't be trusted. There's no peaceful co-existence with people like that." I scratched a red spot on my arm and opened *Climax.* "The sadistic face of the Red Army Colonel broke into a fiendish grin as he looked at the naked body of the captive American girl."

"This is how I like to see American girls," he said. He raised the whip.

"You know," I said to my friend, "I missed all this when I was over the other side. Nothing like this happened to me. Maybe it's because I wasn't a proper tourist. Do you think they put these shows on specially for the visitors who travel in groups?"

"Most likely," he said. "Most likely."

"Do you think people read these comics seriously?"

"Some," he said. "Some."

●

"Do you think they make comics like this in Russia with the Americans as the villains?"

"Maybe. It's all propaganda."

"I don't like being told who I've got to hate. Do you?"

"No."

"And it's happening all the time. You've got to be on your guard. You've got to be on your guard all the time. That's the only way; else you've had it—and it's small pieces of gold and vodka again."

We wandered away from the shop of combats and climaxes.

"How does it feel to be back in England?"

I couldn't answer the question. I was glad to see good friends again but I'd be glad to see them anywhere and all this talk of ways of life of different countries seems nonsensical to me. The world's a big place and we're all big enough to live in it. Or meant to be big enough—

"O Jesus wept and well he might!" A woman cursed as a car on the road threw a puddle of rain over her—

I decided to go home and headed for the railway station.

●

The White Bus

$\mathcal{T}$he boy walking in front of me stopped all of a sudden. He was listening to a football match broadcast on a transistor radio. The match ended. He carefully switched off the radio and hurled it to the ground and started to jump on it and he didn't stop jumping until the instrument was a heap of broken plastic and colored wires.

"Didn't your side win then?"

"Sod my side. They couldn't win if they were matched against a team of old-age pensioners."

He carefully scraped his mashed radio off the pavement into the gutter.

"I hope my bad language didn't offend you. But that team's supposed to be representing England. I think

●

165

they're in the pay of a foreign power. Bloody hell! We must be the laughingstock of the world. I think this country's had it. It can't do anything well any more. Mediocrity. That's what we're exporting. Mediocrity. Horizontal heavyweights and O sod it!"

He walked away and I started off again toward the railway station. The night before I had traveled down to London on a football special—a midnight train specially laid on for football fans. I knew that the train I was now going to catch would be full of the same fans returning. I sat down in an empty carriage and watched men and boys and young girls and old women decked out in England's colored favors traipse through the ticket barrier. One woman was dressed from head to foot in Red White and Blue. A boy wore a striped top hat four feet high. A dead-march.

"O Jesus what will become of us in the European Cup?"

"O Mother."

"I've never felt so shamed—"

"I won't put my money on 'em again not likely—"

"Right through his legs—that ball trickled in slow motion right through his legs—"

"Bowlegged bugger—"

The British Railways Puffing Billy headed north full of sighs and accusations. But just as victory has its obligations so does defeat and it wasn't long before a tidal

●

wave of beer was washing through the train. Men went to the bar and returned carrying full crates, glasses and bottle opener.

"Catch!" they said and threw the bottles into quick hands. It wasn't long before somebody started to sing.

*"The pale moon was rising above the green mountains
The sun was declining beneath the blue sea . . ."*

I was handed a glass. I knocked back the contents thinking it was water. It was gin. The boy in the four-foot-high striped top hat bent down toward me and smiled—I saw his teeth and never before and never since have I seen a mouth with so many teeth in it so big and so white. He filled my glass.

"Drink up. This is stolen property."

"Are you really a thief?" I asked him.

"Not really. I've never nicked anything off my own bat but I've often assisted in the nicking thereof."

We emptied the bottle between us and when a porter muffled up to the earholes in cap overcoat and scarf knocked on the window and shouted "All off you're home!" we didn't believe it.

"We've not been on this train four hours and a half. They're trying to lose us."

"This is probably some wilderness like Cheadle Hulme or Chorlton-cum-Hardy—"

●

"—or Maiden-head," the boy said and giggled—

"Or Middle-sex," I giggled back. We both roared laughing.

"No, it's us."

"Come on then. I'll give you a hand—"

We helped each other out of the train, and outside the railway station he stood with his mates at the bus stop—

"Which way do you go, love?"

"Opposite way to you."

"I'll see you home."

"I only live round the corner. Is this your bus?"

"Yes."

"You'd better get it. It's the last one before morning."

The men took off their silk rosettes and pinned them to my coat.

"You wear 'em. Might bring us a bit of luck next time. Good night, love."

Left alone I leaned against the bus stop. It had been a cold day. It was turning out a colder night. Most people were indoors soaking up heat from high-stacked fires but outside in the open the air was sharp enough to cut yourself on and I stamped the frosting ground for warmth and muttered, "Hurry up, bus. Get a move on." Thirty-five nuns well wrapped up against the weather entered the railway station.

"The Lourdes Special will leave from Platform 8 at eleven-thirteen."

●

The Station Announcer sneered over the broadcasting system. An ancient crone looking more dead than alive, a crucifix clasped in her twisted hands, was pushed in a wheelchair toward the Lourdes Special. She was followed by a procession of cripples on crutches in wheelchairs on stretchers. They came cared for by priests and nurses and nuns and monks. I stopped one of the priests.

"Excuse me, Father, but do you really believe in miracles?"

"I do, my child."

"Well tell me this—have you ever known a man with one leg come back from Lourdes with two? I mean one miracle's as easy as another, isn't it?"

"You mock me, my child, but bless you all the same."

"You're very free with your blessings, Father."

He smiled and the procession disappeared. "O hurry up, bus," I prayed. "Don't let me stand here much longer or I might get carried off to Lourdes, too." In answer to my prayers a white double-decker bus came round the corner and pulled up in front of me. The Lord Mayor, wearing the rich robes and regalia of his office, stood on the platform. Behind him the Mace-Bearer slouched. The Lord Mayor spoke.

LORD MAYOR

I am a plain man. I was born in this city. I played in its streets barefoot. Today I am worth three-quarters of a million pounds. This spirit of enterprise is typical of this city. Go-ahead, tolerant and decent. Recent publicity however has dwelt on the less savory aspects of life here. We all know that slums exist here. We all know that there are some unhappy and unfortunate people here. We know we have a certain amount of prostitution and so on and so forth. But these things exist in all great industrial cities and we see no reason why our share of these unfortunate social ailments should be made so much of. We heads of local government therefore have decided to throw the city open to the public. You are invited to see your city as it really is—a decent place inhabited by decent people. We have much to be proud of. Our past—often cruel and unjust—has fashioned our present. We have looked often into Hell—unemployment—exploitation—two wars have robbed us of the flower of our manhood. But let us not linger in the past. Let us see what the fires of hunger and poverty have forged. A fine race of people. A people set apart—noted for their warmth and friendliness—their hard-headedness and overwhelming hospitality. You are invited to visit all local government offices—education, welfare, the fire service—our cultural organizations will be putting on shows for you—our male-voice choir and symphony orchestra will be giving many recitals—the art gallery will be displaying a life-size reproduction of a street in this city as it was one hundred years ago—within

●

170

the next three weeks the city's first professional repertory theatre will be opened. This theatre has an interesting history. Originally a theatre opened by Sir Henry Irving himself it was then with the coming of talking pictures turned into a cinema. Five years ago it closed and since then has been used as a storehouse. Two months ago I purchased the property with the intention of re-opening it as a theatre. Gloomy folk have said that it will fail. They point out that theatres are closing all over the country through lack of support. They say I will lose money. But I believe that there are enough intelligent people in this city to turn our theatre into a thriving place exciting and progressive. I have invested a lot of money in this scheme. The money does not interest me so much as I am more on the cultural side. The first production will be *A Kiss for Cinderella* by J. M. Barrie. We look to you for patronage. These special white buses have been bought to take residents and foreign visitors on conducted tours of the city—we want you all to see that this place is not solely a collection of miserable slum dwellings—which do exist but which are rapidly being demolished. New homes are rising in their places —homes which anyone can be proud of—

MACE-BEARER

Hurry up—

●

171

LORD MAYOR

So step aboard this SEE YOUR CITY BUS—and see your city as it really is—

The Lord Mayor sat down and the Mace-Bearer helped me mount the bus.

The Lord Mayor turned to me and said, "Aren't you that girl—the one who writes?"

"Yes, I am," I told him.

"Writing all this sexy stuff about this city. Unmarried mothers and things and homosexuals— You've given us a bad reputation in the eyes of the country, you know. If you must write there's better things to write about than that sort of thing. Clean decent things. I've read what you've written. It's hot stuff, isn't it? Do you write from experience?"

"All the time."

"You've made a lot of money I shouldn't wonder."

"Yes."

"I'm old enough to be your grandfather, you know."

"I know."

"I'm worth three-quarters of a million pounds, you know. I'd like to take you out to supper sometime and talk to you. I could give you some very sound advice which has served me well in the past. You're very unpopular with some people in this city, you know. But I'm more tolerant. Ever since I saw you on television

●

172

I've been wanting to meet you. I've met a few theatre
people. They've always been very broad-minded. I'd
like to tell you the story of my life. It's good material
for a book—you writers are always on the lookout for
material, aren't you? You don't mind my talking to you
in a paternal way, do you, but you're very young and
could easily make a few mistakes . . ."

"That's very kind. Would you stop feeling my leg
please?"

I moved away and sat down beside the Mace-Bearer.
Soft music sounded. A Voice came over the air.

VOICE

We welcome you aboard this SEE YOUR CITY BUS and
hope that your journey will be a comfortable and happy
one. Coffee and biscuits will be served at the halfway
stage in our journey. If you wish to smoke, please sit on
the top deck.

The bus driver revved up the engine and we were
away.

VOICE

We are now traveling at twenty-five miles an hour in
an easterly direction. You will notice we are gradually

leaving the heavily built-up industrialized area of the city and approaching more open country. Many of our more noted citizens live here in these pleasant detached houses. On the left you will notice Queen Oak Park— once known as Shaftesbury Park after the great nine-teenth-century reformer who did so much to alleviate the suffering of children. The name was changed after Her Majesty the Queen on a recent visit to the city planted two oak trees there. The park is a popular place in summer—

MACE-BEARER

I was conceived there under a rhododendron bush— by the duck pond—

VOICE

—especially amongst the less fortunate members of the community who have no gardens of their own as yet. It offers many attractions—apart from enjoying the beauty of the trees and the flowers people can also play golf on the miniature golf course and tennis—and of course the ducks on the pond are always popular. Next to the park we have one of our three hospitals. This is called Hope Hospital. It was originally built as a work-house. The hospital facing it is for incurables and we are

●

justly proud of the work that goes on there. The large mansion house coming up on the right is now a girls' school. Originally it was the home of the famous Armington family—

The Mace-Bearer whispered down my ear, "Built by Josiah Armington, one of them that made a good screw out of the industrial revolution—Bloody Josiah—

VOICE

Josiah Armington founder of the Armington Empire was a man who combined great business acumen with Christianity and humanity. The Armington Miners' Rest Home still stands as a symbol of his interest in the welfare of the men who worked so hard to make him one of the wealthiest men in the world. He also started the Armington Domestic Prizes Scheme, a scheme which flourishes to this day. The Committee awards ten prizes of £2 to wives widows and spinsters who have resided here for three years and do their own housework. The prizes are given for the best kept and cleanest home—income and number of children being taken into consideration. Applicants are visited by Committee Members. In Josiah's day Armington Hall was the mecca of the cream of English Society. The Industrial Revolution served Josiah well and he never forgot the debt he owed

●

to his workers. Once a week he threw the Hall open to the public and free of charge the mill workers and miners, their wives and children, could roam at will through their master's home viewing his many priceless treasures—some of which he bequeathed to the city museum. Armington evenings—their balls and musical recitals—were glittering occasions that enriched many lives. Imagine the spectacle! The Hall illuminated from top to bottom—the finest orchestras—the finest food and wines—elegant ladies and their escorts dressed in the finest clothes swirling on the dance floor—alas those days have gone but the Hall still serves a useful purpose in its capacity as a high school for girls.

"Did you go to school there?" the Mace-Bearer asked me.
"Yes."

VOICE

Next door to Armington Hall a boys' school has been built . . .

"When the boys' school was opened," I said to the Mace-Bearer, "the teachers at the girls' school got dead worried. Our headmistress made a new rule—all the girls had to come to school quarter of an hour before the boys,

●

176

and we had to leave quarter of an hour earlier too so there was no chance of us meeting— They even turned down a request from the boys' headmaster that we should form a two-sex Drama Group—"

"My daughter used to go there—before your time though—she did very well out of it too. Married a Yank. She used to take a suitcase to school every morning and for months I thought, That girl's studying very hard if she needs a case to carry all her books in. Then I found out the case was full of cigarettes and nylons and contraceptives that she was flogging to the other girls—"

"O I've heard all about her. She's a legendary figure. Her exploits are handed down from one generation of schoolgirls to another."

"She was a bugger."

VOICE

Both the boys' and girls' schools have fine academic and sporting records. And now we are approaching the Central Library where any book can be borrowed free of charge. Its stocks are kept as up-to-the-minute as possible—

LORD MAYOR

They have some disgusting books in there. I recently borrowed one written by a former Member of Parlia-

SWEETLY SINGS THE DONKEY

ment who was imprisoned for many years on account of his unorthodox practices in business.

Did you, sir?

LORD MAYOR

In this book he mentions a clergyman who was sentenced to ten years for perversion. I had no great sympathy for the clergyman but after borrowing other books from the public libraries in this city I began to think the sentence was hard. Most of these books which I selected at random were proselytizing tracts for homosexual practices disguised as literature. I won't mention the titles of these books for obvious reasons. One of the authors of these books which I selected at random is in my opinion, after looking up his background, a person who sooner or later will come into collision with the authorities. In the meantime he is free to write filthy books and have them published at great profit. Anything he writes is acclaimed by the critics. This author maintains that public revulsion at perversion is a middle-class prejudice. Most alarming. I am wondering how many more dirty books there are in our public libraries. Such literature can only lead to the stimulation of such practices. I can tell you an anomaly from my own experience. I used to work for a printer who employed women in the machine rooms. One of these women called another a name which though not exactly dirty was vulgar and unpleasant. She was dismissed on the spot— At that very moment I was reading aloud to the head printer the most incredible mishmash in the style of the late D. H. Lawrence with all the four-letter words such as at one time were only displayed on the walls of public lavatories—

VOICE

Ahead of you you will see the local gasworks. It is not generally known that this city was the first place in the world to provide gas for the public-at-large at nominal charges. On the left we have the local government offices —education recreation and welfare work all stem from these buildings and you are invited to inspect them at your leisure. An interesting thing about the welfare departments in this city is that though no record is preserved of the paid health visitors, we do know that it was first of all the results of voluntary effort on the part of wealthy and influential ladies and closely connected with religious work. The *Manchester Mission Magazine,* dated January 1860, carried an advertisement for, and here I quote, "an earnest woman for the purpose of selling Bibles and doing any other good for which oppor-

●

179

tunity may arise to advance the domestic welfare and spiritual instruction of the most degraded and destitute, especially women." In the next issue in April 1860 the woman had been appointed and good results were claimed though only the results of religious evangelization are reported. Another woman was appointed to this work the following year and the management of it was handed over to an Association of Ladies entitled The Female Bible and Domestic Mission. These Bible Women distributed among other things cards relating to infant management and also took charge of the patterns of baby clothing which had been prepared with the help of the Ladies' Sanitary Association. These cards were made somewhat ornamental so that they could be hung up in cottages and appealed to whenever their assistance was required.

These tracts were entitled as follows—

About to Marry
Wedded Life
Wedded Life Lost and Found
The Sick Child's Cry
Something Homely
The Mischiefs of Bad Air
The Power of Soap and Water
The Cheap Doctor
Never Despair

Whose Fault Is It?
Why Do People Hasten Death?

The Movement flourished—in the Annual Report of the
Ladies' Sanitary Reform Association for 1872 we read,
and I quote, "disinfecting powders and medical soap are
the keys by which the doors and hearts are opened . . .
the poor are most grateful for the agents' visits . . . in
all these cases the mission woman has been superin-
tended and more or less accompanied by a lady . . .
large quantities of disinfectant have been distributed
. . . been noticed that districts in which this has been
done the most have been unusually free from fevers and
other disorders . . . it cannot be known what good has
been done by the powder alone in prevention . . ."
Little did those women know what a great thing they
were planting the seeds of. . . .

LORD MAYOR

Hear hear.

VOICE

In this city each individual is cared for from the cradle
to the grave. On the left you will see one of the newly
built Children's Homes which is run in conjunction
with the National Society for the Prevention of Cruelty
to Children—and coming up on the right The Home-

●

stead, a beautifully appointed Old People's Home—we are noted here for our care for the aged—no other city can boast as fine a record in this sphere as this one can—

LORD MAYOR

Now we're coming towards the Zoo—that was my idea —we've never had a zoo in this city—

The Mace-Bearer sang softly to himself:

> *"That's the way to the zoo*
> *That's the way to the zoo*
> *The monkey house is nearly full*
> *But there's room enough for you."*

"Don't be rude," I said to him.

> *"Toorally oorally oorally oo*
> *They're wanting monkeys at the zoo*
> *I'd apply if I were you*
> *And get a situation."*

LORD MAYOR

It's very popular especially with the kiddies. It's full every day with sightseers.

VOICE

We are now heading towards the center of town where

we will stop for a while in our journey and have re-
freshments—

The bus pulled up outside a café. A notice in the café
window read Coach Parties and Foreign Visitors Welcome.

"You'd think this was Montmartre or something,
wouldn't you?" I said to the Mace-Bearer.

"In the eyes of some it is."

We left the bus and headed toward the café door. The
pubs were shutting up shop for the night and a man
singing as if his belly was full of nightingales made his
way home. In the café we were handed coffee and biscuits. The Mace-Bearer took my biscuits and stood above
me.

"Open your mouth," he ordered.

I did so.

"Put out your tongue."

I put out my tongue and he placed the biscuit on my
tongue muttering loudly in Latin. The Italian waiter
turned pale and crossed himself.

"I'm going," I said to the Mace-Bearer, "before there's
a fight."

I fled from the shop feeling sick all of a sudden. The
gin I had drunk on the football train started to curdle in
my stomach. I leaned against the graveyard wall. The

graveyard is hidden now under weeds and wild grass and in summer it is covered with yellow dandelions. I slouched against the crumbling wall feeling sick and full of pity for myself. The gin-tears slopped down my face.

"I know just how you feel, love. I know what it's like to lose a loved one."

It was an old man talking. He was watching me and his face was full of sympathy.

"But you're young. You'll get over it. But better to let the tears out instead of keeping them corked up inside you. I've three brothers buried here. And my mother too. Aye, I've seen 'em come and I've seen 'em go . . ."

I tasted the gin in the back of my throat and wondered why he hadn't gone too. I retched and howled at the same time. When I opened my eyes again the old man was moving away. I suddenly felt the ground hard beneath my feet and I looked down. I was standing on a flat black stone let into the ground. I jumped off it. Who had I been standing on? Kneeling down I scraped the frost and the dirt away and read the faded inscription.

ERNEST TITTERINGTON

1834———1854

HE SOUGHT A CITY FAIR AND HIGH

●

I reckoned up. Eighteen thirty-four to eighteen fifty-four? How many years is that? Not long. Hardly anything when you come to weigh up. I walked away from the old graveyard. He sought a city fair and high, did he? In his twenty years did he find it?

To get to where I lived I had to walk through a part of the city that was being demolished. Part of the demolition had been done but whole rows of evacuated houses had been left standing waiting for the bulldozers. Shop signs creaked. It was like a ghost town in a cowboy picture. Windows had been smashed and doors removed. I saw uncarpeted stairs and empty rooms. All around this deserted place the new city sheered up higher than ever before. Not so far away I saw the top half of the tallest building ever raised in England. A jet plane coming in to land at Manchester Airport circled overhead and cargo ships maneuvering the great canal sirened and heavy night traffic careered along the main road that skirted the half-cleared area I was wandering in.

"Go on, let me."

"No."

"I thought you liked me."

"I do like you."

"Then why won't you . . ."

"Because I feel so daft!"

A girl ran out of an empty house and a boy stood in the doorway watching her go.

"Stupid girl, what you go and do that for?" he said and punched the wall with his fist and then ran away himself sucking his scraped fist. A solitary chip-shop on the corner with a poster announcing its imminent demolition pasted to the window closed its doors for the night. The chip-shop man turned to the chip-shop woman and said, "Time for bed, my love."

"Time to clear the place up, you mean," she answered and handed him a sweeping brush.

"O my love," he protested, "I'm tired. It's been a long day. Let us leave this work and go to rest. We can clear the mess up tomorrow."

But his wife ignored him and started to scrub reciting as she did so, "If we don't do Saturday's work till Sunday we won't do Sunday's work till Monday we won't do Monday's work till Tuesday we won't do Tuesday's work till Wednesday we won't do Wednesday's work till Thursday we won't do Thursday's work till Friday we won't do Friday's work till Saturday and we'll never catch Saturday's work again."

And the man, soon intoxicated with the rhythm, set himself to polishing and sweeping the condemned shop and I went away—murmuring.